"What do you think?" Kelly ventured.

What Jase thought was that some clever female had latched on to his father and was trying to take him for a bundle, but he had the good sense not to say so. In the corporate world he wasn't known for his tact or sensitivity; however, both seemed necessary here, so he kept silent.

"He seemed like such a nice man," Kelly muttered. "I never thought he'd do such a rotten thing."

"Who?" Jase asked absently.

"Your father. He really had me fooled. I thought he was great. So great that I set him up with my mother. My *own mother*. And what does he do? He kidnaps her!" She glared at Jase. "Is he on drugs?"

The look he shot her could have ignited a stick of dynamite a mile away. While he was practicing forbearance, she was aiming straight for the jugular!

Dear Reader,

Although our culture is always changing, the desire to love and be loved is a constant in every woman's heart. Silhouette Romances reflect that desire, sweeping you away with books that will make you laugh and cry, poignant stories that will move you time and time again.

This year we're featuring Romances with a playful twist. Remember those fun-loving heroines who always manage to get themselves into tricky predicaments? You'll enjoy reading about their escapades in Silhouette Romances by Brittany Young, Debbie Macomber, Annette Broadrick and Rita Rainville.

We're also publishing Romances by many of your all-time favorites such as Ginna Gray, Diana Palmer and Joan Hohl. Your overwhelming reaction to these authors has served as a touchstone for us, and we're pleased to bring you more books with Silhouette's distinctive medley of charm, wit and—above all—*romance*. I hope you enjoy this book, and the many stories to come.

Sincerely,

Rosalind Noonan
Senior Editor
SILHOUETTE BOOKS

RITA RAINVILLE
The Glorious Quest

Silhouette Romance

Published by Silhouette Books New York

America's Publisher of Contemporary Romance

To David and Stella—
Two special people, friends as well as family.
Happy twenty-fifth!

SILHOUETTE BOOKS
300 E. 42nd St., New York, N.Y. 10017

Copyright © 1986 by Rita Rainville

ISBN: 0-373-08448-X

First Silhouette Books printing August 1986

America's Publisher of Contemporary Romance

Printed in the U.S.A.

RITA RAINVILLE

grew up reading truckloads of romances and replotting the endings of sad movies. She had always wanted to write the kind of romances she likes to read. She finds people endlessly interesting, and that is reflected in her writing. She is happily married and lives in California with her family.

Chapter One

Kelly Lyndon believed in getting over rough ground as lightly as possible. And as quickly. Which is why she was sitting in her Oakhurst office early on a hellish Tuesday morning—which had followed an equally hellish Monday—watching a silver BMW slide to a halt in the small parking lot of Vacationland Kennels.

He didn't look happy, she decided gloomily, as the door swung open and a man loomed head and shoulders above the car. Of course, she hadn't really expected him to. After all, she *was* ruining his vacation. Or, at the very least, putting quite a strain on it. But it was all his fault, she reminded herself bracingly. His dog had been registered under false pretenses.

Friendly, his wife had told Mike when she left the sleek boxer. The dog was friendly and sociable. She had neglected to mention that it was also equal parts kangaroo and Houdini. There wasn't a fence the fiend hadn't climbed or jumped over; there wasn't a locked gate that he hadn't eased through with the stealth of a cat burglar. Once he was out, he romped around with idiotic amiability, visiting the other inmates and driving them into a frenzy of high-pitched, vocal jealousy.

Kelly watched with resignation as the screen door settled with a pneumatic sigh behind the grim-faced man. There was something ominous about a large, angry man, she thought, blinking at the height and breadth of him. And when he's very large and very angry, she decided, he could be downright intimidating.

She walked slowly over to the oak counter, hoping that he would mistake her hesitation for composure.

"Kelly Lyndon?"

"Yes."

"Where is he?" His voice was quiet and deep, with a tinge of frost that was obviously temper.

"Out in back."

"Exactly where in back?"

Kelly gestured over her shoulder to the rear door. "Locked up in the isolation room."

The man stiffened. "Will you tell me just why in sweet hell you have him locked up?"

"Because," she pointed out in a reasonable tone, "I can't control him unless I do. He breaks out every chance he gets."

"So you lock him up?" he asked, looking down at her in disbelief and obviously struggling with several strong emotions.

"Of course! What else can I do?" Kelly raised questioning blue eyes to her visitor. He stood with his back to the light and she squinted, trying to make out the color of his eyes. She gave up after a moment, distracted by his next question.

"Have you thought of just letting him go?"

Now it was her turn to stare in disbelief. Obviously the man had never run a kennel. His suggestion was the stuff of nightmares. She shuddered at the very thought.

"If I let him go," Kelly began slowly, as if teaching a simple lesson to a blockhead, "just because he seems to be—"

"*Seems*? I'd say that climbing fences and picking locks was more than an indication—"

"He didn't exactly pick the lock," she protested. "It was more like—"

"I'm not going to argue about semantics," the man's deep voice overrode hers. "I just want—"

Apparently neither of them was going to complete a sentence, Kelly concluded, as a plump woman burst through the door.

"Where's my bill?" she gasped.

"I beg your pardon?" Kelly's voice was as blank as her expression as she surreptitiously eyed the woman's flushed face. In her experience, people rarely beat down the door demanding to settle their accounts. Such enthusiasm was usually reserved for inspecting their pampered pets.

"My bill," the woman repeated in a shrill voice. "I demand to see my bill."

Casting a harried glance at the large, dark-haired man, Kelly murmured, "If you'll just tell me your name, I'll find—"

"You've *lost* my bill?" The slowly uttered words were filled with horror.

"Of course not," Kelly soothed. "Just tell me your—"

"Where is my bill?" the woman interrupted, her voice sliding up to a screech. "My Wilberforce!"

Kelly did some rapid mental calculations. Wilberforce, otherwise known as Wily Willie, the leaping boxer. Obviously Bill, not bill. But if the panting woman had come to collect Willie, she wondered, slanting a perplexed look at the simmering man, who was *he*?

Five minutes later the prancing dog was led out the door to the accompaniment of agitated clucking. "Poor Bill, we never should have left you! Next time, if we—" The stream of assurances was cut off by the slam of a car door.

Kelly turned back to the man. He hadn't changed a bit. He was just as tall, just as angry and just as intimidating. He also seemed to have taken root. He hadn't moved one of his considerable number of muscles. Not that she could see them under the dark suit, light blue shirt and silk tie with a dash of maroon, but the man had the rangy grace and easy movement of a natural athlete. A swimmer or a runner, she decided.

She perched a hip on a high stool and wiggled until the rest of her shapely bottom covered the seat. "I give up," she said, glancing up at a well-tanned face that seemed composed entirely of strong lines and angles.

"Obviously you're not here to collect Willie. Who did you think I had locked up?"

His neatly trimmed mustache gave a reluctant twitch. "My father."

Kelly stared at the man before her. He topped six feet by several inches. His dark-brown hair, casually brushed back, was a bit long, considering the conservative cut of his expensive suit. He looked, she decided, like a renegade disguised as a well-dressed businessman. But a disciplined renegade, fully in control of himself and whatever he chose to take on.

"Why would I lock up your father?" she asked in astonishment. "I don't even know him. As far as that goes, I don't even know *you*."

Before he could respond, she went on. "But that's beside the point. Even if I did know him, I wouldn't do that. In case you haven't noticed, this is a kennel. I lock up dogs, not people. Of course," she added thoughtfully, "that's not to say that the world might not be a better place if dogs were allowed to run free and a few more people were locked up, but my business license doesn't allow me to make such decisions."

Her eyes met his and some nagging familiarity brought her to a halt. "Who are you?" she finally asked.

"Jase Whittaker, and my father is Matthew L. Whittaker..."

At her blank expression, the deep voice recited a list of credentials that should have been, and probably was, in *Who's Who in America*.

"...and the president of Whittaker's in Fresno," he ended.

Kelly drew in a relieved breath, pleased that she could set his mind at rest. She didn't know the president of the Fresno Chamber of Commerce, much less one of an international conglomerate. "I've never heard of him," she assured him.

Her answer did not elicit the response she expected. She blinked at the sight of his black scowl. His hard voice matched his words; words that were riddled with doubt and suspicion.

"According to the report of my private investigator, he visited this office several times, and he was last seen on Saturday evening with your mother."

Private *investigator*? He must be kidding. She slanted a quick glance up at him. He was serious.

Kelly's gaze shifted to some distant point over Jase Whittaker's shoulder. Last Saturday? Two vertical frown lines formed between her brows as she mentally replayed last week's conversation with her mother. Actually, she decided after a few moments, it had been longer than that—nine, no, ten days ago.

A week ago last Saturday, Abby Lyndon had stepped into the kennel office patting the perspiration on her forehead with a tissue.

"Good Lord, Kelly, how can you stand this heat?" she asked, dropping down on a wooden bench. In faded jeans, a tank top and tennis shoes, she didn't look much older than her daughter.

Kelly had looked up from the paper she was scrutinizing and grinned. "Not all of us can have posh offices in an air-conditioned building."

"You call the cigar box I work in posh?"

"It's close. It has carpeting and a walnut desk. Anyway, if you get that promotion, you'll have a bigger and probably colder one."

"If," Abby repeated glumly. "That's why I'm here."

"You came to the wrong place," Kelly told her mother. "I don't have any clout with Mr. Dever. Besides, if he saw you dressed like that," she pointed at the jeans that clung so faithfully to Abby's shapely legs, "he'd think twice before he made you the first woman vice-president in his precious company. He might start lusting after you, though," she added thoughtfully. "Would that help?"

"God forbid," Abby said piously.

In the silence that followed, Kelly watched her mother's vivid face. Abby's present position at the Fresno-based insurance company was nothing short of a series of major miracles, she decided for the hundredth time. Ten years before, Mr. Dever, in an attempt to prove that he was an equal-opportunity employer, had decided to add a woman to his staff. Abby, newly widowed, frightened and subdued by the responsibility of raising a teenage daughter by herself, had applied. Mr. Dever, looking no further than her adequate qualifications, colorless voice and expressionless face, hired her. That was the first miracle.

The second was that Abby was good at her job.

The third was a bit harder to define. What it boiled down to, though, was that Mr. Dever had never realized that Abby was a very attractive woman. As time had passed, Abby's pain had receded and the life force within her reasserted itself, bringing zest and beauty back into her life. By that stage, however, Mr. Dever, a most pragmatic man, had accepted her as an efficient, asexual extension of himself. His only concession to her gender was a mumbled "Mrs." when he introduced her.

To give credit where it was due, Abby was an active participant in her own transformation. Or lack of it. She deliberately kept a low profile. Not, Kelly doubted, that Mr. Dever would have noticed if Abby sprouted another head—as long as she worked like a drudge and maintained an output equivalent to any two other employees'. But Abby's understated business suits and brisk air kept Mr. Dever a happy man. She had even found a nice, colorless man named Arnold who escorted her to all the company's social functions and was satisfied with a platonic friendship.

The other miracles, too numerous to count, neatly conspired to help Abby restrain her sense of the absurd during the work week and keep her out of Mr. Dever's path on the weekends.

"So tell me why you're here," Kelly prompted. "Is Mr. D. being a bigger pain than usual? You want me to sic one of my dogs on him?" she asked with a grin. "I've got one that would love to jump his wrought-iron fence and romp around in his garden."

Abby scowled thoughtfully at her scruffy tennis shoes. "Arnold's in Europe."

"Good for Arnold," Kelly said promptly, not particularly surprised by Abby's verbal leap. "You want me to send him a postcard?"

"No. I want you to get me a date."

Kelly eyed her mother in round-eyed amazement. "Really?"

Abby nodded.

"Right away?"

"For next Saturday."

"I don't believe it," Kelly stated, eyeing Abby in suspicion. "I've nagged you for years to get on with your life, to find another man. Why the big rush all of a sudden?"

"The annual company dinner-dance."

"Oh, God, Mom, not another one of those awful, deadly things."

Abby nodded again, not denying the insipidity of the event. "As a potential vice-president, I have to be there. And I need an escort."

"What about—"

"Arnold's in Europe," Abby repeated.

"Oh, yeah."

"What do you think? Can you do it?"

"I don't know any Arnolds," Kelly warned.

Abby sighed and glanced briefly, pleadingly, at the ceiling. "I'm not asking for a carbon copy. I'm not even asking for Prince Charming. All I want is a man who looks presentable in a tux, can hold up his end of a conversation for a few hours, work his way around the dance floor without too much trouble and won't fall into that ghastly ceremonial punch bowl. Is that asking too much?"

"Well, I don't know," Kelly said, straight-faced. "At your age, you can't be too picky."

"Forty-three isn't exactly pushing senility," Abby began. After a quick glance at the gleam in Kelly's eyes, she sighed sharply and leaned back. "When will I learn?" she muttered.

"How many years have I been trying to—"

"Kelly, don't start. I've heard that lecture so many times I can quote it verbatim. Yes, you've been playing matchmaker for more years than I want to remember. No, I haven't cooperated. I haven't wanted a man in my life on a permanent basis. I don't now."

She held up her hand, palm out, as Kelly opened her mouth. "Watch my lips," Abby directed, speaking slowly. "All I want is an escort for the evening. Understand?"

Kelly bit back a smile and nodded.

"If I promise to change," Abby asked solemnly, "will you help me?"

Kelly tilted her head and eyed her mother speculatively.

"I'll become a punk rocker," Abby promised. "Or some rich man's plaything. I'll even run away with a gigolo. I'll do anything if you'll just help me find a date for next Saturday."

"Promise?"

"Promise."

Soft laughter filled the small room. It came from two slim throats but sounded surprisingly alike. In fact, everything about the two women was similar. Abby had been most generous when passing along her genes, a friend had once commented. Kelly stood an inch taller than her mother's five foot five, her blond hair a bit lighter, her blue eyes a shade deeper. She appreciated the bonus of larger breasts but moaned about the additional inch on her hips. Both women had mouths that were a bit too wide, high cheekbones and too-square faces softened by vulnerable jawlines. Neither was beautiful; both had an inner quality that reassured women and intrigued men. Both were also oblivious of this fact.

"All right," Kelly said in a businesslike tone, "let's get to work. We've got to find you a man, right?"

"For the evening," Abby qualified.

"Someone who can hold his own with your professional crowd," Kelly murmured, sinking into a thoughtful coma.

Abby watched hopefully. "Do you know someone?"

"I . . . think . . . so."

"What's his name?"

"Matt."

"Matt what?"

"I don't know."

"Just how well do you know this guy?" Abby asked suspiciously.

"He's easy to talk to," Kelly offered.

"How long have you known him?"

"Just a few days," Kelly admitted. "But he's really nice. I met him when he helped me corner Wily Willie last week."

"Who?"

"I told you about him, remember? This crazy boxer I'm trying to keep corralled?" She waggled her hand impatiently. "Anyway, he got out, Matt saw me chasing him and helped. After I got him under lock and key—"

"The dog?"

"Right. Matt hung around and visited for a while. He came around several times after that, just to talk.

"Doesn't he have a job?"

Kelly shrugged. "He didn't talk about himself very much."

"I don't know," Abby said skeptically. "He seems to have an awful lot of time on his hands. Don't you know *anything* about him?"

Kelly's sigh was one of pure exasperation. "What do you want just for an evening? He's a perfect candidate. He's tall, has dark hair that's graying, warm greeny-blue eyes and no paunch. In fact, he's in darn good shape for, ahem, a man of his age. And," she added as a clincher, "he's intelligent and charming. He may or may not have a job, but believe me, he's no bum."

"All right." Abby's reluctance couldn't have been clearer if she had scribbled her doubts on the gleaming wooden counter separating Kelly's desk from the reception area. "Do you think he'll want to do it? Do you suppose he has a tux?"

"He'll do it," Kelly said with certainty, not about to let her mother back out at this point. "But I doubt if he's carrying a tux around with him. You may have to spring for the rental fee."

"No problem," Abby said absently, clearly having second thoughts.

Kelly had made several excuses to get rid of Abby. If her mother's expression was any indication, they were as unbelievable as they were hasty. But they did the job. Abby went on her way before she could think of any other complaints and Kelly looked for, and found, Matt.

Actually, he found her. He dropped in for a visit several hours after Abby left. Kelly informed him that he was an answer to her prayers, explained the situation, tactfully slid in the bit about providing him with a tuxedo, and rested wide blue eyes on him as she waited for his answer.

Matt seemed entertained by the whole thing, but agreeable. However, he stated firmly, he would supply his own tuxedo. He got Abby's address, confirmed the time and left.

Kelly had called Abby, informing her that she couldn't back out. Everything was set.

The dinner-dance had taken place last Saturday; today, one of the items on her agenda had been to call her mother.

Now, gathering the loose ends of her thoughts into a tidy bundle, Kelly looked once again at Matthew L. Whittaker's son.

"Matt?" she asked him dubiously. "Are we talking about Matt?"

"No one," Jase stated unequivocally, shifting to lean an elbow on the counter, "ever calls my father Matt."

"That settles it then. We can't be talking about the same person," Kelly said decisively. Then she looked up into a pair of cold, greeny-blue eyes and knew that she was wrong.

A startled gasp caught in her throat and became an agitated cough. Although why she was surprised, she decided, as a strong hand reached over the counter and efficiently whacked her on the back, was beyond her. If she had had her wits about her, she would have seen the resemblance as soon as Jase walked through the door. But she hadn't and she didn't.

For one thing, his eyes, now that he was no longer backlit by the open door, were a dead giveaway: they were almond shaped, beneath familiar dark, thick, peaked brows. He was taller than Matt but both men shared a loose-limbed grace; an easy, effortless way of moving that hinted at a reservoir of agile strength. Odd qualities for desk-bound men to have, she thought idly, a fleeting picture of the two of them in white tennis shorts bounding over a net to congratulate their opponents. Wrong, she decided, mentally erasing the image. At least, if the losers did the bounding. It took more than her fertile imagination was capable of to picture Matt or Jase Whittaker as losers—at anything.

Backing away from the ministering hand, Kelly cleared her throat and wiped her eyes. She looked up with a watery frown into fierce eyes that were momentarily more green than blue. "I'm sorry to hear about Matt," she said carefully. "Is there anything I can do to help?"

"Given the fact that your mother is also missing, I damn well hope so."

"*What?*" Kelly's eyes locked on his expressionless face.

"Your mother," he repeated. "Missing."

"No, you're wrong." She shook her head, ignoring the blond tendrils of hair that broke loose from the long thick braid hanging down her back and clung to her cheeks. Glancing at her watch, she said, "Two hours ago, my mother left her home in Fresno, walked a little over a mile to Dever's Insurance building and settled down to work. She's no farther away than that."

"Do you know that for sure?"

Nodding, Kelly said, "She always follows the same pattern during the week."

"When did you last see her?"

Kelly sighed. By the tone of his voice, he wasn't going to give up easily. Well, she decided fairly, she wouldn't either, if Abby were missing.

"Ten days ago."

"When did you last talk to her?"

"Last Friday. And Sunday she left a message on my answering machine. She said everything was fine, and she'd talk to me in a day or so. I was going to call her this afternoon."

"Why don't you try right now?"

Kelly felt a flutter of alarm stir in her stomach and move upward to compress her lungs. Nothing had happened to Abby. She was certain of that. Bad news always traveled fast. If Abby were ill or missing, she would have been notified. She was absolutely positive. Almost.

"Now?"

He nodded. "Now."

"Uh, afternoons are better. I always call then."

Jase leaned over the counter, stretched out a long arm and lifted the telephone from her desk. He plunked it down on the counter and handed her the receiver. "*Now*, Kelly."

His expression was now determined. His eyes, the set of his shoulders, every inch of his six-foot-plus frame told her he wouldn't budge an inch until she made the call. Glaring up at him, she snatched the telephone, poked out the number and listened as it rang three times. In the midst of the fourth buzz, a calm voice informed her she was speaking to a representative of Dever's Insurance Company, Mrs. Lyndon's office.

"Marge?" she said to Abby's secretary, "this is Kelly. Can I speak to Mom, please?" She tapped a neatly-filed, unpolished fingernail on the counter, expecting to be connected. She almost dropped the receiver at the secretary's reply.

"What did you say?" she asked in a too-calm voice.

"What did she say?" Jase asked, nudging her hand.

Waving him to silence, Kelly's eyes grew round as she listened.

"Did you forget that she's on vacation?" Marge repeated.

Vacation? But it was only June. Early June, at that. Abby never took hers until at least August. She maintained that early-summer vacations were equivalent to none at all, saying that those who returned in July and did everyone else's work all summer needed another vacation by September. And she would *never* leave without telling Kelly.

"Oh, uh...yeah, I...guess I did," Kelly finally managed.

"Kelly? Is anything wrong?"

"No. Nothing at all," she said quickly. Abby wouldn't thank her for alarming Marge and sending waves through the Dever grapevine. A large, tanned hand tilted the receiver away from her ear. Jase leaned forward so they both could hear.

"Oh. For a minute there, you sounded funny."

Kelly made an indeterminate sound that simultaneously soothed and encouraged Marge.

"I suppose you've talked to Abby since the dance?" she asked.

"Well, no," Kelly admitted. "Actually that's why I'm calling now. I forgot she'd be at home," she added hastily.

"Good," Marge said with a giggle. "I'm dying to tell you."

Giggle? Marge? Kelly eyed the counter blankly. Abby's secretary was in her fifties—a nice woman, but extremely professional and entirely too serious. She had worked for Abby three years before she relented and called Kelly anything other than Miss Lyndon. Kelly had no reason to believe that the woman even knew how to giggle.

"Tell me what?" Kelly asked cautiously.

"About her performance at the dance."

Kelly raised her eyes to Jase's expressionless face. "Performance?"

"I think perhaps she had a bit too much to drink."

"Mother?" Kelly's brows almost met her hairline. She had never known Abby to have more than a couple of glasses of wine. "What happened, Marge?"

"But, then, maybe not," Marge stated, obviously continuing her train of thought. "Unless she started drinking before she got there. But she looked different when she walked in."

"How different?"

"For one thing, her hair was down."

"Down?" Years before, Abby had decided that a chignon struck just the right professional touch. She had never since attended a business function with her hair styled differently.

"And her gown was . . ." The words dwindled away to nothing.

"Was *what*?" Kelly held the receiver in a stranglehold.

"Well, I just never realized that she had such . . . I mean I've never seen her look so . . . It's not that it was too . . . It was blue," she ended flatly, as if that covered everything.

"Blue?" Kelly repeated, stunned. The infamous blue dress? The one Abby had vowed she would never wear? Mother and daughter had been on a shopping spree when Kelly spotted the dress, and strong-armed Abby into buying it. There was really nothing wrong with it. It didn't have a slit to the thigh or a neckline cut to the waist. It was elegant and designed to make a woman feel and look like a woman. But it was definitely not the kind of dress Abby wore to a Dever dinner. It was, Abby had said wistfully as she hung it at the back of her closet, a dress to wear for a man—a special man.

"Okay," she said carefully. "Mom came in looking different. Go on."

"No," Marge corrected. "Not yet. Part of her different look was the man with her."

Kelly felt the telephone jerk as Jase tightened his grip.

"It definitely wasn't Arnold," Marge said in satisfaction. "Matt, uh, Whitney, I think, was his name. And thank God for that. Arnold never would have handled things the way Matt did."

"What things?" Kelly asked in a hollow voice, trying to pull the receiver closer to her ear.

"Like whipping off a tablecloth to wrap around your mother," Marge replied.

Kelly examined the large, tanned knuckles so close to her own. "Why did he do that?" she asked reluctantly.

"Because she fell in the punch bowl."

Kelly blinked.

"Not really fell in," Marge continued in a reassuring voice. "Just sort of tripped and dunked in an elbow."

"How did that happen?"

"Well, Mr. Dever was so surprised when Matt told him he was a pompous fool that he flung out his arm and hit Abby. She stepped back, lost one of her shoes, and that's when it happened."

"But, why did Matt—" Kelly began feebly.

"Because Mr. Dever told Abby that they shouldn't have won the dance contest."

Kelly looked wildly at Jase to see if he was making any more sense of the conversation than she was. If his expression was any indication, he wasn't.

"Who shouldn't have?" she finally asked.

Marge spoke with exaggerated patience. "Matt and Abby. Aren't you listening, Kelly? The other couples had been practising for months, and those two just walked away with first prize. Mr. Dever argued with the judges, then started on Abby. I thought Matt was going to deck him," she ended with relish.

Kelly mumbled her thanks and dropped the receiver. Blue eyes met aquamarine.

"My father doesn't do exhibition dancing," Jase said flatly.

"And my mother doesn't fall in punch bowls!"

Chapter Two

Matt?" *Abby's husky whisper broke the silence of the star-sprinkled darkness. They stood alone on a dark carpet of dewy grass in Yosemite Valley, well beyond the muted lights falling from the windows of the Ahwahnee Hotel. She shivered as his lips brushed her cheek.*

"Hmm?" He closed his teeth gently on her earlobe, blood singing in his ears as her heart slammed against his.

"Why?" she asked, sliding her arms around his neck.

"Why am I running away with you?" Matt's hands brushed down her body, settling at the base of her spine, pressing her closer. "Why am I crazy about you? Or why am I letting you keep me out of your bed—for the time being?" He settled one more kiss on

the damp earlobe before investigating the sweet curve of her shoulder.

"All of the above, I guess," she mumbled, tilting her head to give him better access. "But especially the first."

"Because," he said, propping his chin on her head, smiling as a strand of blond hair clung to his cheek, "you opened your door to me and I found the magic that I lost more than fifteen years ago. And," he reminded her, "in a weak moment, you told me you felt the same way." His arms crossed behind her, holding her a willing captive.

Abby touched his warm throat with her lips. "What if it doesn't last?" she asked in a shaky voice.

Matt's grin was a defiant slash of white in the darkness. "That's why we're here by ourselves, love. And why we'll stay away until all your doubts disappear. We'll go back when you know it'll last, and not one minute sooner."

"Sounds wonderful," Abby mumbled against his chest. "But..."

"Hmm?"

"I'm worried about Kelly."

"She'll be okay."

"How do you know?"

"I've got a plan."

Abby raised her head. "What?"

He shook his head, lowering his mouth to hers. "Later," he said.

"I'll find him," Jase said grimly.

"Where are you going to start?" Kelly asked.

"With your mother."

Kelly glared at Jase's broad shoulders as he walked out the door. Maddening man. Not a bit like his father. Her eyes gleamed with satisfaction as he slammed the car door and gunned the motor. Nasty temper, she decided. It would serve him right if he ended up with ulcers. Totally unreasonable, she concluded, as he made a screeching right turn and disappeared from view. If Matt decided to go away and sow some wild oats, or whatever men did at his age, how on earth was Abby to blame? One blind date, for heaven's sake. That's all they'd had.

Pulling the telephone closer, she poked the familiar numbers. "Marge? I forgot to—"

"Kelly! Why did you hang up?" Marge didn't wait for an answer. "I wasn't through. Where did Abby *find* that man? He was absolutely gorgeous! The perfect answer to midlife crisis. Lean and hungry-looking."

"Hungry? Weren't they there for the dinner?"

Marge made a disgusted noise, muttering something about kids. "He never took his eyes off of her, Kelly. He reminded me of a starving man being led to a banquet." She ended in a romantic sigh.

In the silence that followed, Kelly stared at the counter as if it were a crystal ball. Abby? Her mother? A banquet?

"And I wish you could have seen them dance," Marge went on. "Nothing flamboyant, you understand, just smooth and...sexy."

Kelly cleared her throat. "Sexy?"

"Definitely," Marge agreed, repeating the word with satisfaction. "At first, while I was watching them, I thought I was having a hot flash. But, if I was, so was every other woman in the room.''

"Uh...yeah," Kelly mumbled, trying to visualize her mother giving anyone a hot flash. "When did she tell you about her vacation plans?'' she finally inquired.

"As they were leaving. It was certainly a surprise to me. She hadn't said a thing about it before the dance. She just told me that she was going and she'd take care of the paperwork when she got back." Marge laughed softly. "Mr. Dever's having a fit."

So was she, Kelly admitted to herself an hour later. So was she. Abby was not answering her telephone. Apparently, if she wanted to corner her elusive mother, she would have to drive the fifty-odd miles down the mountain to Fresno. And she would do precisely that, she decided, as soon as Mike walked through the door.

Mike Trent was her cousin, best friend and partner. They had grown up on the same street in Oakhurst. They had attended the same schools, separated only by his two-year seniority. Kelly was fifteen when her father died and she moved "down the hill" to Fresno with Abby. But before the move was made, she and Mike planned their future.

A kennel was exactly what the town needed, they had decided. Not an ordinary, run-of-the-mill kennel, though—a special one to fit the particular needs of Oakhurst. The city, they believed, had been providentially located for their purpose. The southern tip of Highway 49, a well-traveled road for those interested in the Mother Lode countryside, meandered to a standstill near the center of town. The Bass Lake resort area was just a few miles to the east and the southern entrance to Yosemite National Park was a short drive to the north.

And what was so special about this central location? they had asked each other with wide grins. What did it mean to them? Tourists. Lots and lots of lovely tourists. Tourists who would flock to the area and rent hundreds of cabins and hotel rooms. They would find accommodations that were comfortable, charming and convenient—and prohibited animals. For the people who would not leave their pampered pets at home, Vacationland Kennels would be the answer.

And so it was. After getting off to a shaky start, it was now beginning to pay its own way. Visitors who needed to have their dogs within petting distance greeted the advent of Vacationland with cries of jubilation. And what was even better, they spread the word to friends who were similarly afflicted. They also paid half in advance.

Mulling over this satisfactory state of affairs, Kelly almost overlooked Mike's arrival. Almost. But Mike was not a man easily overlooked, she decided with a grin. He was big—football-big—with shoulders like a brick fence, and strength to match. He had terrorized entire football teams while in college, she remembered. He was still pretty intimidating—if you didn't know him. Among his large circle of friends it was an open secret that Michael Allen Trent was the softest touch in town.

"Hi, Mike." Kelly watched as his sandy hair skimmed the top of the door frame.

His large hand gently tugged at the end of her long, silky braid. "Hi, babe." He looked down with a teasing grin. "Get rid of Willie?"

Kelly's sigh was loud. "Someone has to be the bad guy around here," she pointed out. "If you had been here, we'd have probably ended up with the monster for another month."

"Probably," he admitted, his smile growing wider. "Anyone else come in?"

"Yeah, but not with a dog." For the next five minutes Kelly told him about Jase Whittaker and her conversation with Marge. "You met Matt," she ended with a rush. "What was your impression?"

Mike closed his mouth with a snap. "Aunt Abby?" he asked, an intrigued expression in his hazel eyes. "A *banquet?*"

Kelly shrugged and widened her eyes in an expression that clearly said, "Beats me!" She prodded his shoulder with a slim finger. "Matt," she repeated firmly. "What do you think of him?"

"That he'd be hell on wheels if he wanted to be. What's his son like?"

"A younger, grimmer and tougher version of Matt," she said succinctly, frowning at his answer. "Probably also hell on wheels. Mom isn't answering her phone," she said abruptly. "Will you take over while I drive down and see if I can find her?"

Mike perched on a corner of the desk. "What if you can't?"

"What do you mean?"

"Don't play stupid," he advised. "What if she's gone? With Matt?"

"She wouldn't do that," Kelly said with absolute conviction. There was no denying that her mother was an attractive woman; she had always been proud of Abby's looks. But banquets and hot flashes? Really!

Besides, in the mother-daughter dialogues that had stretched out over the years, the one thing Abby had been absolutely adamant about was premarital sex. She had freely admitted to regarding the subject with tunnel vision, but that hadn't softened her outlook. Sex, she had stated too many times to be counted, was not a happening; it was a commitment—to love and to life. If dimples, muscular shoulders and a cute tush happened to accompany it, so much the better. But the operative word was *commitment*. Kelly had listened and reluctantly agreed. Which accounted for the fact that she was probably the only twenty-four-year-old virgin left in all of Madera County. Was she now to believe that her mother, after one date, had skipped out the door and fallen into Matt's bed? Hardly.

"Can you think of any other reason she'd disappear without telling you?" Mike asked with devastating logic.

"We don't know that she's gone any farther than the grocery store," Kelly pointed out. "She could just be running some errands."

"But just suppose it's more than that?" he asked with maddening persistence. "What if she's really gone with him?"

"Then I'll just go find them and bring her home," Kelly declared fiercely. "It's all my fault, if she did. I set her up with Matt. I'm the one who nagged her about her dull life. I'm the one who pushed until she threatened to run away with a gigolo," she groaned, her active imagination conjuring up images of white slavery and drug-induced orgies.

"Now listen, Coyote," Mike began.

"Don't 'Coyote' me," she said, bristling at the name. It was one he had pinned on her years before, after they saw *The Man of La Mancha.* He had—with surprising perception for one so young—compared her to the idealistic Don Quixote, even if he had mangled the name. She was, he'd insisted, always trying to right wrongs and loved nothing better than setting off on wild goose chases. But there was nothing the least bit glorious about a useless quest, he'd repeatedly informed her as the years rolled by. The fact that his reminders were usually delivered as he rescued her from various situations of her own making didn't make them any less annoying, she acknowledged.

Now, warding off another lecture, she grabbed her purse and headed for the door. "I'll find her," she promised, "or know the reason why."

Five hours later in Bass Lake, Kelly sat in her living room scowling at her diet drink. The room was light and airy, with gleaming wood floors, area rugs, a floral print sofa and caned chairs. Thriving green plants and bright splashes of persimmon made it a cheerful, comfortable room. But now, kicking off her sandals and dropping down restlessly on the end of the sofa, she was neither cheered nor comforted.

She had not found Abby, and she knew why. Abby was gone. Her house was locked up tighter than a fortress and her neighbor, Ellen, was sending her son over to water the grass. Ellen had found an envelope tucked in her door Sunday morning. It contained a house key and a note from Abby saying that she was taking a trip and requesting that her lawn and plants be kept alive.

Kelly stretched out a leg, nudging a honey-colored mop of hair with her foot. A nub of a tail feathered the carpet in response.

"What do you think, Annie?" she asked the dog. "Where should I start looking for Mom?"

A depressed sigh shuddered through the animal.

Kelly looked down in fond disgust, kneading the dog lightly with her toes. Annie had the soft floppy ears and soulful eyes typical of a cocker spaniel. She was the laziest dog in the county, and had obviously been elsewhere when a canine deity allotted intelligence. She was highly suspicious of butterflies and had once been traumatized by a confrontation with an irate clicking beetle. However, when she decided that Kelly was being threatened, her disposition changed to that of an enraged, slavering Doberman.

Another gloomy sigh tapered away to a muffled groan.

"Exactly," Kelly agreed. "That's how I feel when I wonder if there's a chance that Jase Whittaker might be right."

Ignoring a third doleful moan, she tried to objectively examine the sparse facts at her disposal. First, Abby was missing; second, so was Matt... and that was it. The rest was pure conjecture. Without one shred of evidence, Jase had decided that they were together. Coincidentally, Marge, with an evening of observations under her belt, had arrived at the same conclusion. And what was worse, Kelly admitted to herself, even she couldn't think of any other reason for

Abby's disappearing and neglecting to leave a message for her.

Following the logical train of thought from her mother to Matt, Kelly soon arrived at Jase—and wished she hadn't. He was a far cry from the men she usually associated with. A little older—early to mid-thirties—and far too serious. No, actually, "grim" was the word. He looked as if he spent too much time frowning at financial statements and underlings and none at all at having fun. There was nothing malleable about him. He was undoubtedly a man who knew exactly what he wanted—and exactly how to get it.

What disturbed her the most, Kelly finally admitted, was the expression in his eyes. Beneath the legitimate concern and irritation was a blatant male speculation that shook her to the core. It reminded her of something Marge had said. She shook her head to dissolve images of hungry men and banquets. No. Absolutely not.

But those aquamarine eyes with a deep-turquoise rim around the irises had assessed, resolved and served notice. He would clear up this mess, they had mutely informed her. Then, when he was through, he would return. And when he did, she decided, taking a swallow of her drink and almost swallowing an ice cube, it wouldn't be to discuss boarding a dog.

And why did that bother her? For one reason, growing up with Mike and his friends had almost convinced her that she was one of the boys. Oh, things had changed a bit as her body assumed feminine contours—but not an awful lot. When she began dating, Mike hovered protectively in the background, and there wasn't a young man around who would risk having his neck separated from his shoulders.... So there had been years of camaraderie, but no passion.

Each year, when the flatlanders invaded for the summer, she enjoyed the influx of new men but recognized the transience of those associations. She tilted her head, thinking of some of those dates. Nice men, but none were special. Dining, dancing and swimming were pleasant pastimes, but she had realized somewhere around her nineteenth birthday that a lasting relationship rarely developed in two or three weeks.

Recently she had been giving herself pep talks and deciding to do some serious looking for a man. Just the week before, hadn't she reminded herself that she was twenty-four? Almost a quarter of a century old? What she needed was a nice, amiable man who would receive Mike's stamp of approval and fit into the small-town atmosphere she preferred. He would be an affable husband and indulgent father to their two children. He would move into her cozy mountain home in Bass Lake and they would all live happily ever after.

He would definitely not be arrogant and intimidating. Nor would he tower over her and plunk phones down in front of her and insist that she make calls when she didn't want to. Warming to her subject, she decided that he'd have blond hair, or maybe red— certainly not dark. And he definitely wouldn't have a mustache.

Having settled that to her satisfaction, Kelly leaned back with a sigh of contentment. Life was really quite simple when you took it firmly in hand. All that was necessary was a specific plan and determination.

Annie raised her head and stared at the telephone. Kelly had never become accustomed to the unnerving instinct that allowed the dog to sense when the instrument was about to peal. Unaware that a fate that hated twenty-four-year-old contented virgins was on the move, Kelly reached out to answer the ringing phone.

"Hello?"

"Kelly?"

She recognized the deep, slightly gritty voice immediately. "Who's this?" she asked.

"Cute," Jase said dryly. "Did you find your mother?"

Kelly stared at the wall. She would gladly have sacrificed her new ice-pink sundress and tossed in the potted palm out on the deck if she could have given an affirmative answer. "No," she told him baldly.

After a prolonged silence, he asked, "What do you intend to do now?"

Her fixed gaze became a glare. "You're the one with the private detective and all the ideas. What do you suggest?"

She had the impression that he was carefully selecting his next words.

"That we join forces."

She waited. When it was obvious that he was waiting for her reaction, she drew in a sharp breath. "You mean you want to...?" Her words dwindled away as she realized that she didn't know *what* he wanted.

"I mean," he said impatiently, "to try to work this thing out together."

"Why?"

"Because," he said in an exasperated voice, "you are, presumably, as concerned about your mother as

I am about my father. If they're all right, one or both
of us should be hearing something. The only logical
thing to do is pool what information we get."

"I suppose you're right," she said reluctantly after
a moment's thought. He was, of course. But the last
thing she wanted to do was play Watson to his
Holmes. And she didn't doubt for a minute that it
would end up that way. The few minutes she had spent
with him earlier that day had made an indelible
impression. When Jase Whittaker was around, he was
in charge.

"Good." His voice was brisk. "I'll come by the
kennel about one tomorrow. We need to talk."

"Wait a minute," she said hurriedly, before he
could hang up. "I made arrangements to run some
errands tomorrow. We'd better make it some other
time."

"I don't have any other time," he said after a short
pause. "I'll drive you wherever you need to go. We
can talk in the car."

Kelly listened to the dial tone for a few seconds,
mumbled in irritation and slammed down the receiver.

"Where next?"

Kelly pointed a neatly manicured finger straight
ahead. "That way."

Jase sighed, aimed his silver bullet and stepped on
the gas. They had been on the road for an hour and
had stopped more times than he could remember. So
far they had visited an antique store that was doing a
thriving business despite its location on a narrow dusty
road. He had listened to a husband and wife squab-

bling cheerfully as they selected colors for a stained glass window and watched a young mother as she casually produced flowing calligraphy on delicately tinted parchment. On the sun porch of an old house, a gray, gaunt man had squinted through thick glasses as he wove an intricately patterned rug on an old hand-loom. Farther down the street, in an ancient garage, a short brawny man with hands like hams had shaped exquisite ceramics. And they all greeted Kelly as if she were bringing sunbeams after a month of rain.

He glanced down, eyeing the gentle swell of her breasts not quite concealed by the rounded neck of her sundress. "Why didn't you tell me you were cramming two days' work into an afternoon?"

"You hung up before I had a chance," she pointed out in a reasonable tone. It served him right, she thought. If he had waited a few seconds last night, she would have explained about the local arts-and-crafts show she was coordinating. It was scheduled for mid-July and she had three million last-minute details to arrange. "The last stop is out that way," she said, waving to the right. "Go north on Highway 49."

He waited for the light to change, then veered right.

"Some day I'm going to take a couple of months and follow this road all through the Mother Lode country," Kelly said. "The romance of the gold rush has always fascinated me."

Jase slanted a sardonic look down at her dreamy expression. "The miners worked standing in the hot sun or up to their knees in icy water," he said conversationally. "They probably had sunstroke or frostbite most of the time. Then there were the thieves and con men—"

"But just think of the color, the excitement," Kelly murmured.

"And the dust and sweat, rain and mud."

"The dance halls and music."

"The miners hardly ever struck it rich," he reminded her. "The saloon keepers set up business, sometimes with no more than two barrels supporting a plank. They made fortunes. Then the merchants moved in. They also made a bundle. A slice of bread cost a dollar. Two if buttered. A shovel cost fifty."

"That's downright depressing," Kelly said in disgust.

"But true."

She scowled at his profile. "I'll bet you could turn Cinderella into a Greek tragedy." She straightened at the sight of a familiar landmark. "That's the house, over there."

Jase came to a stop near the front porch, watching as a couple in their forties came down the steps to meet them. Their expressions lightened as Kelly called a greeting.

"Hi, George. Emily. This is Jase Whittaker. Jase, the Hardings."

Two minutes later they were all holding tall glasses of freshly squeezed lemonade and were examining George's polished wood carvings.

"George, they're super," Kelly assured him, running her finger down the delicately carved profile of a child. "But they always are. Will you have plenty for the show?"

George nodded calmly as they walked back to the car. He held the door for Kelly, closing it when she was settled. "We saw Abby the other night," he said casually. "She's looking good."

"Mom? When?" She was aware of Jase stiffening beside her.

"When was it?" George asked, looking at Emily. "Sunday? Or Monday?"

"Monday," she replied, slipping her arm around his waist.

"You sure?" He dropped his hand on her shoulder and waited.

Jase took a deep breath. Before he could open his mouth, Kelly reached back and pinched the taut flesh of his thigh. He jerked but kept still.

Emily nodded. "Positive. Because Sunday was Candy's birthday and we went to her party. Remember?"

George thought a minute. "Yeah, that's right." He looked down through the open window at Kelly. "Monday evening. That's when we saw her."

It was an effort, but Kelly kept her voice casual. "Where were you?"

"Up at Yosemite. At the Ahwahnee. Having a drink out on the patio."

Kelly eyed the two of them suspiciously as they exchanged amused glances. "And, uh, what was Mom doing?"

The corners of George's mouth kicked up in a grin. "Well," he said carefully, "I'm not sure, but I *think* it was the Mexican hat dance. On a table."

Kelly's mouth fell open.

"It was kind of hard to tell, you understand, because there was quite a crowd around her," George continued, with a broad smile.

Kelly cleared her throat. "Was she alone?"

Emily giggled and took up the story. "I don't think so. There was this man standing close by. He was clapping his hands to the music and cheering her on."

"Did you know him?" Kelly asked weakly.

"Nope. But he knew her. Or if he didn't, the gleam in his eyes said he soon would. Nice-looking man," she added. "Tall, with dark hair going gray. In fact," she said, bending over and peering in the window, "he looked enough like Jase to be his father."

Chapter Three

Abby slid off the horse into Matt's waiting arms. His hands closed around her waist as if they had been custom-made to fit that particular curve of her body.

A radiant smile answered his lazy grin. "Oh, Matt, what a wonderful day. I've had such fun." The words ended in a strangled gasp as he lowered her, an inch at a time, brushing the tips of her breasts down the broad expanse of his chest. Her stunned gaze rose to meet the challenge of his as her feet touched the ground.

Matt gave her a quick hug, then released her before his body betrayed his determined control. He had sworn that he wouldn't rush her, damn it. She needed more than five days, and she'd get it—even if it killed him. And it probably would, he reflected grimly, draping an arm around her shoulders and turning her to walk down the path beside him, hip to hip, thigh to thigh. He had had his share of women over the empty years, but never one whom he wanted to throw over his shoulder and kidnap. Never one whose softness he wanted to find flowing over his body each morning, who would fill his arms each evening. Never one who made his body throb like a teenager's.

Matt was still amazed at how quickly it had all happened. By the time he had taken Abby home after the company dance, he had made several decisions. First and foremost, she was his woman. He would erase the cool, self-contained executive persona that the Devers of the world had stamped on her and bring out the vibrant, whimsical woman who lurked so seductively behind the blue, wide-eyed gaze. He understood her uncertainties. He would be patient.

He was aware that in the business world he had a reputation as a shrewd, deliberate man. A methodical man. A man who set his sights on a target and got exactly what he aimed for. Although he was acting with uncharacteristic haste, he intended that this situation would be no exception.

The silence in the car, as it wound its way back to Oakhurst, was all but palpable.

"What do you think?" Kelly finally ventured, looking at the rigid profile of the man beside her.

What Jase thought was that some clever female had latched onto his father in a vulnerable moment and was trying to take him for a bundle, but he had the good sense not to say so. A muscle contracted in his cheek as he bit back the words. In his corporate world, he was known neither for his tact nor his sensitivity; however, at this stage of the game, both seemed necessary.

Jase frowned, two deep vertical lines furrowing between his brows. It was apparent that Kelly would fly to her mother's defense at the flicker of an eyelash. He shot a quick glance at her. Loyalty was a quality he had always admired, but in her case it was definitely misplaced. Her mother was obviously a... A quick glance at her apprehensive blue eyes settled it. He'd wait. He needed more information, but he'd tread lightly. No point in hurting an innocent bystander—if that's what she was. The jury, he reflected, was still out on that point.

"He seemed like such a nice man," Kelly muttered. "I never thought he'd do such a rotten thing."

"Who?" Jase asked absently.

"Matt."

The word exploded in the car with all the delicacy of a boulder roaring down a cliff into a bubbling mountain stream.

Jase's fingers tightened on the steering wheel, sending the finely tuned car skittering into the next lane. "What the hell are you talking about?" he half snarled.

Kelly glowered at some distant point through the windshield, blind to the tense features of the man beside her. "He really had me fooled," she said bitterly. "He helped me with Willy and came by to visit. I thought he was great. So great that I set him up with my mother. My *own mother.* And what does he do? He kidnaps her!" Turning sideways in the bucket seat and glaring at Jase, she demanded, "Is he on drugs?"

Jase's brows snapped together over his straight nose. The look he shot her could have ignited a stick of dynamite a mile away. So much for kid gloves, he thought grimly. While he was practising forbearance, she was aiming straight for the jugular.

The ride back to the kennels was a silent one. Kelly's expressive features made no secret of her thoughts and despite Jase's wordless state, she was getting an inkling of what was on his mind. Jase drove automatically, his thoughts leaping ahead to the Ahwahnee Hotel, an hour's drive away. After he dropped Kelly off he should be back on the trail. The car rolled to a halt beside the office screen door. He got out and walked around to the passenger side to open Kelly's door.

She was already standing, her pink sundress drifting around her knees, her sandal-clad feet firmly planted on the asphalt driveway. Kelly looked up, trying to judge his mood. It wasn't easy; in fact, it was downright impossible. His face was a polite mask, shielding whatever emotions he was subduing.

"It's been nice," he said with grim courtesy, obviously not meaning a word of it. He slammed her door and headed back around the car. "Give me a call if you hear anything."

Kelly watched as Jase folded his long legs and wide shoulders back into the car with a neat, economical movement. She frowned. He certainly was in a hurry to get away. He had driven her from one place to another all afternoon with the patience of a dozen saints; now all of a sudden he was in a roaring rush. In spite of her less-than-tactful comments, it didn't make sense. Unless...

She yanked the door back open and dropped down on the seat.

Eyeing him with suspicion, she asked, "You aren't by any chance planning to play supersleuth, are you?"

"What do you mean?"

There was a distinct pause before she informed him coldly, "Injured innocence isn't your bag."

He stared down at her enigmatically. "What is?"

"Trouble," she muttered. "Being stubborn and bossy. And going off," she finished with growing certainty, "to check out the Ahwahnee Hotel and leaving me behind."

His blink broke the impact of her accusing glare.

"I knew it! You really intended to go up there without saying a word, didn't you?" Before he could open his mouth, she rushed on. "Join forces, I believe you said? Work things out together? Pool information?"

Jase settled back with an attentive air. Kelly's braid had fallen over her shoulder and rested on the front of her dress, he noted. Rested wasn't exactly the word he had in mind, he finally decided, watching the agitated rise and fall of her breasts. Her cheeks were flushed with irritation and her eyes were a brilliant shade of blue.

"I don't think you even know the meaning of teamwork!"

He turned toward her politely, resting his chin on a fist as her words washed over him. Some women, he reflected, became tongue-tied when they were angry. Kelly obviously didn't have that problem. He wondered what she'd do if he leaned over and covered her pretty lips with his. He was still considering her reaction when she took a deep breath, her last words ringing in the now-silent car.

"You wait here while I go in and tell Mike I'm going with you."

His long look was one of pure masculine inquiry. "And what if I don't? What's going to keep me here while you're gone?"

"This." She snatched the keys out of the ignition, swung out of the car and raced for the office door. She had almost reached it when she felt Jase behind her.

"Mike! *Mike*." She threw open the door and bolted inside. "*Catch*."

With a casual gesture that spoke volumes for his coordination, Mike rose and snagged the flying keys. His hazel eyes flickered in speculation as Jase stepped through the doorway.

"Hi, babe," Mike said absently, fingering her thick braid as she came to a halt near his desk. His gaze traveled from the keys in his hand to the man standing by the door, hands resting on his hips, his open jacket revealing an impressive breadth of chest beneath his white shirt. "You two together?" he asked politely.

Jase nodded. "In a manner of speaking."

Kelly faced him warily across the room. She wasn't fooled for a minute by his relaxed, superbly masculine stance. Beneath the civilized trappings of his dark-brown suit and striped tie, was a man poised for explosive action. The tense atmosphere was not diminished as each man took an unblinking survey of the other.

Drawing in a deep breath, Kelly mentally reviewed her panicked dash from the car. It had begun so innocently. All she wanted him to do was wait for a couple of minutes. It hadn't seemed like an unreasonable request. When he questioned her, though, taking his keys seemed like the swiftest solution. But as soon as she had withdrawn them from the ignition, she realized her mistake. You might be able to reason with Jase Whittaker, you might even be able to persuade him, but she knew now with absolute certainty that you *never* pushed him.

Clearing her throat to relieve the building pressure, she extended her hand and rested it on Mike's bent arm. "Mike, this is Jase Whittaker." Her eyes clashed with an aquamarine gaze. "Jase, my partner, Mike Trent." She didn't volunteer the information that Mike was also her cousin.

Jase pointedly examined the hand resting near Mike's elbow. He slowly shifted his gaze to Mike's face.

Keeping her voice as matter-of-fact as possible, Kelly said to the younger man, "We're driving up to Yosemite if you can handle things around here."

Glancing at his watch, Mike said, "No problem. It's only a couple of hours until closing time. Why Yosemite?"

Turning to face him, she explained, "George and Emily Harding saw Mom at the Ahwahnee last Monday."

"Alone?"

Sternly disciplining her gaze so it didn't drift in Jase's direction, she said, "Maybe." Feeling the impact of two greenish-blue eyes on her nape, she added honestly, "Probably not."

Mike jingled the keys in his hand, watching Jase. "Yours?"

Jase nodded expressionlessly.

Mike lobbed them across the room to Jase, who caught them without a word. "I want her returned in mint condition," Mike informed him.

Jase's voice was dry. "To you?"

"In the general vicinity," Mike said noncommittally.

Men, Kelly thought in disgust as she absorbed the mutual sizing-up that was taking place. Trying hard not to feel like a juicy bone between two hungry dogs, she turned to Jase, her voice brisk. "Ready?"

Something glimmered in his eyes as he silently reached out and opened the screen door. She wondered fleetingly what he was thinking. A moment later, after a second quick glance at his impassive face, she gave silent thanks that she wasn't a mind reader.

"Coyote?"

Kelly came to a halt and glanced over her shoulder into concerned hazel eyes.

"You'll be okay?"

His question, she knew, covered more than the tautly controlled man beside her. It encompassed mothers, daughters, rich men, love and a host of other emotional categories. She smiled and blew him a kiss. "I'll be okay," she promised.

Jase's warm hand settled on her shoulder. "It's getting late."

She nodded and stepped outside.

They entered Yosemite at the south-west entrance. Only once had the silence been broken as the car sped past craggy oaks, graceful pines and a profusion of greenery on scenic Route 41.

"Coyote?" Jase had asked abruptly.

Kelly hesitated for a thoughtful moment before she replied. "Just an in-joke."

"How important is he to you?"

"Mike?" Her lips curved in a small smile. "Very."

Jase stared grimly at the curving road ahead. Even a blind man would have been aware of the affinity between those two. Trent's touch on her hair, his fingers absently sliding down the thick braid had been the gestures of a man traveling familiar territory. And Kelly had tucked her hand in the crook of his arm with a noticeable lack of self-consciousness. She had leaned into him with the natural grace of a woman who knew her touch was welcome.

He stiffened with a sudden realization: there had been affection between the two, even tenderness. And protectiveness on Mike's part. What was lacking was the undeniable awareness between two people when they were lovers.

Reaching up to the visor, Jase pulled out his sunglasses and slid them on. He slanted a thoughtful glance down at the woman beside him. How long, he wondered, would it take her to touch him with the same naturalness? He amended the question. How long would it take her to realize that she was going to end up in his bed?

"You're looking awfully satisfied, all of a sudden," Kelly commented, pleased that he had finally shed his grim expression. "If you've thought of something cheerful about this mess, how about sharing?"

"I'll do that," he promised with a small grin as he pulled into the parking lot. "Later. Right now we have to go snooping."

Minutes later they were staring at up the ruggedly beautiful six-story hotel, admiring the rambling collection of columns and balconies merging with the valley floor and walls.

It took longer than Jase had anticipated to find someone who could answer their questions because Kelly kept stopping to point out stained glass windows and enormous wrought iron chandeliers. He grasped her wrist, preventing an impetuous side-trip to the patio strewn with colorful umbrella-covered tables. "Come on," he muttered. "You can play tourist some other time."

"Where are we going?" she asked, craning her neck to look outside.

He gestured to the reservation desk. "Over there."

"You're not going to find out anything from them." His eyes, she noted, were almost pure green when he was exasperated.

He kept walking, towing her behind. "Do you have a better suggestion?"

"Give me a minute, I'll think of something." She tugged at his hand, pulling him to a reluctant halt. "Honest, Jase, those people are trained to be close-mouthed. They won't tell you a thing."

Gazing up at his stubborn expression, Kelly sighed. Rallying quickly, she persisted, "What are you going to do, tell them that you think your father ran away with my mother and you're trying to run them to ground? I'm sure they'll be delighted to help."

"Cute, Kelly, real cute. I'm simply going over there to ask for my father's room number. Then..." Jase looked down into wide, blue eyes that had suddenly gone blank. "Kelly? Are you okay?"

Kelly blinked and life returned to her eyes. "Jase," she hissed, "did you hear what that man behind me said? *No,* don't look at him! Just listen. He's telling his wife the most fantastic—" Her words broke off as Jase swung her around and marched her to a nearby love seat.

"For heaven's sake, I'll never figure out what he was going to say! Let me *go.*"

Not only did he refuse to release her, he crowded up against her until the backs of her knees hit the cushion and she abruptly sat down. He dropped beside her and clamped his arm around her shoulders to keep her in place.

He shot her a look of disbelief. "For God's sake, Kelly, were you *eavesdropping*?"

She stared at him, dumbfounded. "Of course I was." Her lips curved up in a grin that made her look about ten years old. "I hear some of the most incredible things that way. You simply can't imagine."

"I don't want to."

"If you hadn't pulled me away, you would have heard that man tell his wife—"

"Kelly!"

Her eyes widened in exasperation. "Don't look like that, Jase. I never listen to anything personal. But I've learned about some terrific vacation spots." He relaxed visibly, until she added, "In addition to some fantastic insights on human nature."

He uncoiled his long body, shaking his head when she moved to join him. "Wait here," he ordered, taking a quick look around and obviously deciding that he had isolated her sufficiently. "I'll be right back."

And he was. Kelly watched him approach the desk. His question was short and the response immediate. The clerk shook her head, smiling politely. He asked something else and the woman's smile stiffened. She shook her head slowly from side to side. Jase swung away, his eyes dark with frustration.

Kelly schooled her expression so there wasn't a trace of "I told you so" on it. "No luck?" she asked.

He sat beside her. "I should have handed her a few bucks," he stated flatly.

"You're slipping, Whittaker." Kelly extended her hand and patted his muscular thigh. "Two minutes ago you were bawling me out for being nosy and now you're grumbling because you didn't bribe someone. Besides, it probably wouldn't have worked. She looks like the type who would've yelled for the manager."

His lips curved in a reluctant grin. "Is that supposed to be comforting?"

"Of course!" She surged to her feet and tugged at his hand. "Now can we try it my way?"

"And what way is that? Skulking behind potted plants, listening to private conversations?"

"You're close." She bit back a smile at the look of alarm that crossed his face. Odd, she thought, that a man who was probably as lethal as a great white shark behind his desk would be so uncomfortable following her lead. Or maybe it wasn't, she decided after a moment's thought. He was accustomed to being in charge. His approach to any problem would be methodical and efficient, with all loose ends neatly tied up. He definitely wouldn't appreciate a style best described as impulsive and off-the-wall, depending a lot on instinct and luck. No, that wouldn't appeal to him at all.

"It won't be so bad," she promised. "In fact, all it involves is going out on the patio for a drink and a friendly chat."

"We don't have to sit on the patio to talk," he informed her, "and the last thing I want right now is a drink."

"Then order orange juice, or iced tea," she tossed over her shoulder, heading outside. "Just get me a waiter."

He was very good at that, she decided a few minutes later. Some men, through no fault of their own, could sit in a restaurant for hours being ignored by everyone in sight; others were blessed with an aura of command that jolted every waiter in sight. Jase was obviously one of the latter.

"Would you please try to look like you're enjoying yourself?" she implored, after a quick glance at his skeptical expression. "We're supposed to be carefree tourists, not a delegation discussing world peace."

"That's the famous plan? We play tourists?"

"Part of it. Your role is the hardest. You have to look amiable."

"And when do we begin our friendly chat?"

"You don't," she murmured absently, watching the waiter veer toward their table. "I do. You smile a lot."

He muttered something that sounded like "Arghh." The approaching waiter, obviously one of the summer student employees, cast him a nervous glance. He didn't seem reassured by Jase's smile. She couldn't blame him, Kelly decided, watching him retreat with their order. Jase looked more like a man afflicted with a tic than one enjoying a summer afternoon.

She looked up with a bright smile as the young man returned and placed a cup of coffee before Jase. "This looks like a great place to work," she commented, sliding her iced tea closer.

"You're right about that," he answered with a grin, then cast a cautious look in the older man's direction. Jase's tight smile and cold eyes didn't encourage him to linger.

"Is this the lull before the storm?" Kelly asked the waiter, her gesture taking in the half-empty patio.

He reached for the bill Jase had laid on the table. "Yeah, it'll be pretty busy out here in a couple of hours."

Kelly reached for the ashtray, moving it closer. In the process, she somehow snagged the money.

The waiter withdrew his hand and shifted his feet.

"I worked up here in the park one year," Kelly informed him, absently folding the bill in small sections. Her smile was reminiscent. "Had a ball, too. The weekends were really wild."

"I just started a couple of weeks ago," he volunteered, watching Kelly's fingers. "Everyone tells me that July and August are the busiest months."

Jase shifted in his seat.

Kelly smiled again, carefully pressing the creases out of the money. "Are Mondays still the slowest nights?"

"Yeah, I guess so," he said vaguely. "Except last Monday," he added, brightening.

Jase jerked to attention.

Kelly's foot connected sharply with his ankle. "Big night?" she asked casually.

He grinned. "We had a mariachi group wandering around singing. Some woman started dancing and ended up getting most of the crowd involved. They were one thirsty bunch."

Quickly, before Jase could formulate the words on his lips, Kelly asked, "Does that happen often?"

Shaking his head, he said, "Not since I've been here. If it hadn't been for that lady, I think people would have just listened. But she was..." He broke off with a puzzled frown.

"She was what?"

"I don't know." He shrugged. "Happy, I guess. So was the guy who was with her." He reflected for a moment, then met Kelly's quizzical gaze. "They cost me five bucks," he admitted with a sheepish smile.

Tilting her head in inquiry, Kelly asked, "How?"

"I pointed them out to my girlfriend and said that they were either just married or celebrating an anniversary. She said they weren't."

"And?"

"I bet that she was wrong."

"Well?" Kelly prodded with a grin. "What happened?"

"I learned not to bet with any of the maids. She was taking care of their rooms. Two rooms. Both being used."

Kelly flashed a triumphant blue glance at Jase. Two rooms, she informed him silently. *Two.* So much for his obvious, if unspoken, suspicions.

Turning back to the waiter, she said brightly, "Well, they sound like nice people. I hope they're still around keeping things stirred up."

"Nope. They checked out Tuesday. After the dancing down here, they invited everyone to a party upstairs in the bar after closing hours."

Jase looked in fascination from the young waiter to Kelly.

"Did the whole crowd go?" she asked.

His wide grin turned into a husky laugh. "No. The manager wouldn't rent them the bar or the musicians so they came back down and told everyone the party was off."

"What a shame," she said faintly.

"But they said they were leaving the next morning for a few days in San Francisco. They invited everyone to meet them at the Top of the Mark for dinner."

Chapter Four

Abby stood beneath the canopy of the St. Francis Hotel watching for the silver gleam of Matt's car. Drawing in a breath of sheer pleasure, she smilingly refused the doorman's raised brow and nod toward the taxis lined up at the curb.

San Francisco's Powell Street was brash and noisy, alive with honking horns, clanging cable cars and the wail of a saxophone from one of the ubiquitous street musicians. And from somewhere off in the distance came the faint sound of bagpipes. One car horn, more persistent than the rest, drew her attention. A lean, tanned hand that she would recognize anywhere in the world gestured to her from the window of a gleaming, low-slung car.

Abby stepped forward and bent over to peer inside. "Matt?"

"Hop in," he ordered briskly. "Quick!"

"This is crazy," she protested, trying to quell the laughter bubbling in her throat.

Matt captured her hand after she had settled her forest-green skirt around her knees. "Why?" he asked, working on an expression of innocent inquiry. "I just bought another car. Nothing so strange about that."

A soft sound of mirth escaped her lips. "Just answer one question: Why a red Corvette?"

"Beats the hell out of me," he admitted with a satisfied grin. "It just seemed the thing to do." He placed her hand on his jean-covered thigh and held it there. "Buckle up," he told her, dragging his gaze from her vivid face to the tangle of traffic ahead of them. "Let's try it out."

Jase finally broke the silence. It had been a thoughtful silence, punctuated with looks ranging from baffled fascination to disbelief. Occasionally Kelly was aware of a curious glance that might have come from a scientist asked to identify an alien being. Now, almost back to Oakhurst, he began to ask the questions that he had been methodically arranging in his head for the past forty-five minutes.

"Do you always do that?"

"Do what?" she asked, deliberately obtuse. That was an introduction to a lecture on "The Dangers of Speaking to Strangers," if she ever heard one.

"Talk to people like that?"

She turned the battery of wide blue eyes on him. "Of course! It goes hand in hand with listening in on private conversations."

"Kelly! I'm serious."

"I know. And that's something I've been meaning to discuss with you. You're entirely *too* serious, Jase. If you don't learn to loosen up, you're going to be a candidate for a heart attack in a few years. You're already a perfect example of those Type-A people— brisk, brusque and too busy to appreciate the little things in life."

"Kelly—"

"For instance, do you have any hobbies?" Before he could open his lips, she answered herself. "Probably not. What do you do for fun? Break up labor disputes and discuss mergers?"

"Kelly—" Jase broke off and stared at the road ahead wondering how his proposed comments concerning a young, attractive woman being entirely too trusting for her own good had evolved into a medical discussion of his declining physical condition.

"Did you notice how beautiful the wildflowers were around the hotel?" She shook her head. "I doubt it." Plowing on with reckless abandon, she asked, "Or how the sun silvered the pine needles? Of course not. Or that woman in the short red—"

"Yes."

"Huh?"

"I noticed her," Jase said evenly.

"Oh. Well did yo—"

"Kelly."

His sharp tone stopped her dead in the middle of a word. "What?" She turned, taking a look at his profile. Grim, she decided. The man simply didn't smile enough. She'd have to do something about that. After she found Abby. Of course, once Abby was located, he might not be around to worry about. She wondered at the absurdly depressing pang of loss the thought gave her.

"Kelly, are you listening to me?" Jase's voice was a blend of exasperated amusement and chairman-of-the-board impatience.

She eyed his carved features again. He might as well have "The Boss" tattooed on his forehead, she thought. He was probably used to people snapping to attention, taking meticulous notes of his every word and trotting off to do his bidding. "Not really," she admitted in polite apology when he slanted a curious glance at her.

"I asked if you always talked to people like that," he repeated with what she recognized as characteristic stubbornness. Obviously he would keep on feeding her one form or another of that question until he received an answer.

She settled back with a sigh. "If you noticed, I did more listening than talking."

He muttered something in disagreement.

"Mostly what I did was ask questions," she pointed out. Warming to her subject, she said, "Jase, there are God-zillion people in the world who love to talk. They want to talk. They *need* to talk." She leaned forward, waving a hand emphatically. "And I love to listen, so all I usually have to do is prime the pump and let them flow."

"You didn't ask him one direct question about your mother," he muttered.

She nodded in agreement. "Or your father."

"Another couple of minutes and that kid would have been telling you his blood type and social security number."

"Probably. Sometimes it's hard to turn them off."

His exasperated sigh was close to a snort. With smooth, economical movements, he maneuvered the car around a curve leading to a long downhill stretch. The lights of Oakhurst glimmered in the distance. Driving silently now, he remembered how she had smiled at the waiter and told him to keep the change. "Are you always such a generous tipper?" he asked, his expression one of genuine interest.

Kelly lifted a shoulder in an unconcerned shrug, then frowned, trying to visualize the bill she had absently creased and smoothed out as she talked to the young man. "For all the help he gave us, I didn't think change from a five was so bad."

"It wouldn't have been," he agreed dryly. "But you gave him a twenty.

Kelly gasped and almost choked. After a moment, she laughed softly, pointing out, "You could have stopped me. It's a good thing you're rich, isn't it?" she added blithely, reaching out and patting his thigh. "Just think of it as subsidizing a hardworking kid's education."

Jase laid his hand over hers, holding it in place. He felt her initial resistance before she deliberately relaxed her fingers. He could, he informed himself wryly, quickly become addicted to this woman's touch. Hell, who was he kidding? He already had. Her endearing habit of reaching out and touching was one of the things that he wanted reserved exclusively for himself—in addition to her impulsive warmth, sapphire-blue eyes, and soft, pliable body that was custom-designed to fit against his.

"Here's the office," she said brightly.

She would be furious if she realized how very obvious her relief was, he thought with a rare flare of humor, intrigued by the touch of panic in her voice. She would also be jumping out of the door before the car stopped rolling if she had any idea where his thoughts were leading him.

"Do you want me to follow you home?" he asked.

"Why?" She was aware of a tinge of breathlessness in her surprised question.

His voice was matter-of-fact. "It's getting late."

"For heaven's sake!" She busied herself with the seat belt. "I've lived up here for years. And I'm not the nervous type." Normally. But then she had never spent several hours in a car next to a quiet man with determined eyes who, without saying a word, was telling her a great many things—things that Mike's presence through the years had kept her from experiencing.

She cleared her throat. "How are we going to follow up on the San Francisco information?"

He stood by her side as she unlocked her lemon-yellow Fiat. "We always stay at the St. Francis. I'll give them a call."

She slid in behind the wheel and looked up. "Will you let me know what you find out?"

He nodded, his eyes darkening as he looked down at her. "Tomorrow."

It was as good as a promise. "Tomorrow," he had said. And Jase Whittaker, Kelly thought as she prowled restlessly around her living room, short as he might be on tact and superficial charm, was a man of his word. So why hadn't he called?

Admittedly, it was still early—she had been home from work only long enough to change into some lavender terry shorts and a matching sleeveless top—but surely he knew how anxious she was. She stopped midstride and looked at the tape player on the small table. Had he also found a message on his answering machine? Had Matthew L. Whittaker's voice reached across the miles with words Jase preferred not to share with her?

Kelly touched the tape player with a slim finger, aware of a lingering sense of unease. Earlier, she had come home for lunch, absently prodding the machine into action while she rummaged in the refrigerator for the makings of a salad. She'd lifted some greens from the crisper, jerking as Abby's warm voice filled the sun-brightened kitchen.

"Kelly. I know you're probably worried sick and if the situation were reversed, I'd murder you. But I'm fine, honey, just fine. I'll explain everything when I get back, I promise. You were absolutely right about Matt. He's everything you said he was, and more."

A note of caution seemed to slow down Abby's joyous flow of words. "Uh, I'm not exactly sure when we'll be back. We may go down south for a while, but I'll keep you posted. In the meantime, take care of yourself. And don't worry!"

Now, dropping down in an oak-frame rocker and rubbing the ball of her bare foot over the dozing dog, she thought about the message. There had been an underlying note of excitement in Abby's voice. She couldn't ever remember her mother sounding so...so...what? Carefree? Exhilarated? Happy? Bone-deep contented? Yes, to all of the above.

If she were a true daughter of the eighties, she would leave it at that. She would, now that she had heard from Abby, wish her mother well, take care of her kennel and craft show, and simply wait for the return of the travelers. But, she admitted to herself with a depressed sigh, she was not and she would not. Abby had done too good a job on her for one lousy telephone message to settle her doubts.

Anyway, unless Jase had done an about-face during the night, he would be tracking the two of them every step of the way. And—but only in order to protect Abby from Jase's probable accusations, Kelly mentally assured herself—she would be right beside him.

Annie raised her head and glanced sleepily at the telephone, uttering a weary groan at the effort. Kelly snatched up the receiver. "Hello! Did you find out anything?" Belatedly, she realized she hadn't allowed it to ring.

"Kelly?" Jase's voice was puzzled, but game. "Have you eaten yet?"

"No. What did you—"

"Do you have a barbecue?"

"Yes. What did—"

"Set it up. I'm bringing some steaks. Do you have stuff for a salad?"

"Yes. What—"

"Good. I'm starved. See you in thirty minutes."

Well, she thought crossly, dropping the telephone receiver into its cradle. If that's a sample of his business approach, it's no wonder he gets things done. It lacks a hell of a lot in charm, but there's no doubt that it's effective. With that out of her system, she stomped over to the large, sliding glass door. Most of the homes in the area were surrounded by spacious, redwood decks on which the inhabitants lived until driven indoors by mosquitoes or the cool evening air. Kelly's was no exception. Her deck meandered around three sides and held a comfortable sprinkling of outdoor furniture arranged for conversation or flat-out lazing.

Moving quickly between the kitchen and deck, Kelly wondered what Jase would think of her home. After setting the table outside, she did a quick check of the house. The windows were sparkling, thanks to an excess of energy a few days before. Hastily straightening towels in the bathroom, she ducked into her bedroom and hung up the clothes she had worn that day. How, she wondered for the millionth time, did some people keep their places model-home neat? Hers was clean, but . . . rumpled. In spite of the numerous closets and cupboards, there simply wasn't room to put everything away.

Back in the kitchen, washing lettuce, Kelly's thoughts returned to Jase. Both times she had seen him, he had obviously been dressed for work. The dark suits that fit his muscular body so superbly were as intimidating as the man himself, and she had a sneaky feeling that he knew it. She wondered idly if he wore them to barbecues. Well, she'd soon find out.

At the sound of a car door being slammed, she dried her hands and headed for the front door. She swung it open just as his finger pressed the bell.

"Hi," she said, smiling up at him. Whatever else she had planned to say was forgotten as her gaze dropped to the brown paper bag he was holding. Not that the bag was all that interesting—it was what was behind and below it that struck her dumb.

He wasn't wearing a suit. In fact, he looked as if he had never owned one in his life, or even known that they existed. His blue Western-style shirt was open at the neck and made his shoulders look too wide to get through the doorway. The jeans that hugged his slim hips and muscular thighs had been washed so often they were a milky shade of blue and looked baby-soft. Clothes that fit like that should be illegal, Kelly decided with a blink, her eyes following the fabric all the way down to where it met and partially covered shiny, dark-brown, narrow-toed boots.

Her wary gaze inched back up to find him watching her with interest. "Howdy, pardner," she said faintly. Rallying at the flicker of something in his eyes that could have been amusement, she flung out an arm in a welcoming gesture. "If you're sure your horse is hitched up tight, come on in."

Jase stepped in and followed her. He took his time, checking out some of the books on the shelves, eyeing a hostile-looking pup on the floor, and tilting his head to examine a modernistic painting that looked as if a palette had been flung at it.

"Is it right side up?" he finally asked.

"I think so." Her answer was absentminded. "I gave up trying to figure it out. It's the colors I like."

Jase set the bag down on the brown tiled counter and glanced around appreciatively. The room was pale yellow with crisp white curtains and oak cupboards. It wasn't just the kitchen, he realized. The entire house was a reflection of Kelly. It was feminine without being cloying, and had her own unique brand of warmth and haphazard charm. It also had a slightly…rumpled air that fascinated him. Again, it was much like Kelly—at least, as he pictured her looking first thing in the morning or after being thoroughly kissed: tousled, enchanting and deliciously feminine.

"Have you taken a vow of silence, or are you going to tell me what you found out?" Kelly demanded as she pulled the steaks out of the bag.

"Not a hell of a lot," he admitted, briefly describing the amiable, yet uninformative message Matt had left on *his* machine. "But I'd just as soon have some food in my stomach before we go into it. Can you wait?"

"Barely," she said in a dry voice. "But I learned a long time ago that it's useless trying to pry information out of a hungry man." She held up the meat. "Can you handle this while I get the rest of the stuff ready?"

Jase took the plate and followed her pointing finger outside to the deck. Stepping past pots overflowing with bright flowers, he examined the burning coals and neatly spread the meat on the grill. Frowning at a large cardboard box, he wondered how many hungry men were in Kelly's life.

"Why do you mess with charcoal when you have a gas barbecue out here?" he wondered aloud.

Kelly looked out the window. "Because it's in at least a hundred pieces and I don't know how to connect them. My uncle gave it to me for my birthday two months ago." She stared in frustration at the outsize box. "He forgot that my mechanical aptitude is zilch."

Jase nudged the box with his toe. "I'll do it for you."

"You don't have to work for your meal," she assured him, looking up with a grin. "I wasn't dropping heavy-handed hints. Really. Mike said he'd fix it when he had a chance."

Staring at her through the screen, Jase said evenly, "I said I'd do it."

Kelly surveyed his rugged features, especially the determined set of his jaw. And that, she informed herself, is apparently that. "Okay." She nodded her thanks. "I was just trying to let you off the hook. When?"

"Tonight, after we eat."

"Speaking of which," she pointed to the smoking grill, "are you watching that meat?"

Twenty minutes later, Kelly set her knife and fork neatly on her plate and said, "Tell me about your frustrating day."

Jase leaned back, his large hand fingering the stemmed glass of chilled Chardonnay with masculine grace. His eyes were bright with curiosity. "How do you know what kind of day I had?"

"If you had good news," she said in the tone of one pointing out the obvious, "you'd have told me the minute you hit the door. On the other hand, it couldn't have been too bad, because you don't look upset. You do seem a bit preoccupied, though, so whatever you're chewing over is probably still unresolved."

"Were any of your ancestors burned as witches?" he queried gently.

She grinned. "No magic involved. Just a little basic psychology."

His gaze drifted over her, stopping to absorb the alert intelligence in her eyes. Some of the sharks he did business with would give a hefty bundle to read him as easily as she did, he thought sardonically.

"You're right," he admitted. "What I learned was neither good nor bad. It was more of a confirmation than anything. They were at the St. Francis."

"Were?"

He nodded. "For two days. I also called the Top of the Mark. They had been there."

"In a place that big, how could anyone remember?"

Jase winced. "They topped off a lavish dinner with a four-hundred-dollar bottle of brandy. They won't be quickly forgotten."

Kelly closed her mouth with a snap. "Four hundred dollars?" she repeated faintly.

Lifting his glass in a toasting gesture, Jase said dryly, "When my father decides to live it up, he does it with class."

"Jase?"

Alerted by her overly casual tone, he looked up and caught the flash of concern in her blue eyes before she lowered her lashes. "Hmm?"

There was a distinct pause before she said, "Never mind. It wasn't important." She stacked the dishes with a brisk clatter, reaching out a hand for his plate. Before she could snatch it, his long fingers closed around her wrist like a manacle.

Gently massaging the silky skin on her inner wrist, he said evenly, "Unimportant questions have a way of growing all out of proportion when they aren't asked."

She smiled unconvincingly and tugged at her hand. "It's silly," she assured him. "Not worth bothering about."

His fingers tightened. Not enough to hurt, but enough to convince her that she wouldn't move an inch until his curiosity was satisfied.

"Kelly?"

Deciding that the situation was rapidly getting out of hand, she capitulated with an exasperated sigh. "I just wondered how they were booked at the hotel."

Narrowing his eyes, Jase tried to interpret the expression on her face.

"Under their own names," he told her. "In two rooms. Both used." Exerting just enough pressure to move her closer, he added, "Does it really matter?"

Kelly dropped back in her chair to avoid being tugged around into his lap. "Yes," she said baldly, "it does. Not the way you think," she added, waving him to silence with her free hand. "I don't have any hangups about my mother being a woman." Well, not *too* many, she silently assured herself. "It's more symbolic than anything."

She dropped her eyes to her captive hand. "I know what you've been thinking. My mother isn't a tramp, Jase. Nor is she in the habit of disappearing with men—especially one she's just met." She flashed him a smile that was meant to convince him that none of it really mattered. It failed miserably. "And I know that having two rooms doesn't mean that they're not sleeping together." She shrugged. "Like I said, it's just symbolic."

Jase lifted her hand, bent his head and lightly brushed his lips across her fingers. "I'm sorry, Kelly," he said carefully, "I didn't mean to give you that impression." That, at least, was honest. He didn't want to give her that impression, even if it was exactly what he'd been thinking.

Kelly stared at him, unable to read his impassive face. The blasted man wasn't giving away a thing. Tugging at her hand, this time successfully, she said brightly, "I'll do the dishes while you get started on the monster. How long do you think it will take?"

He followed her with a handful of dishes and a dissatisfied expression. He wasn't going to lie to her, he brooded. And he wasn't going to tell her what he thought. Damn. Silence, unsatisfactory as it was, was probably the best solution. At least for the present.

"A couple of hours," he finally said. "Do you have a screwdriver? And pliers?"

"Yep." Kelly scrabbled through a drawer pulling out a candle, string, market coupons, pointless pencils, a sample tube of shampoo, a nutcracker, a tattered piece of sandpaper, and a two-foot length of chain for a light fixture. "Aha!" She flourished a screwdriver.

He looked down at the small tool and gave an inward sigh. It was larger than the type an optometrist would use on glasses, but not much. "I keep some things in the car. I'll see if I have something bigger."

Ten minutes later, he was sitting in the middle of the living-room floor, surrounded by rubber wheels, various pieces of heavy metal and at least three thousand screws, nuts and bolts. His expression of anticipation reminded Kelly of her neighbor's little boy when he had been given a gigantic box of building blocks.

Annie sniffed at Jase's boots, a low growl rumbling in her throat. Kelly called Annie to her, settled on the couch and picked up the newspaper. Pages rattled as she turned to the crossword puzzle.

"Your dog doesn't like me," Jase informed her matter-of-factly.

"She doesn't know you."

"Does she growl at Mike?"

"She wouldn't dare," Kelly said, smiling. "He gave her to me."

"She'll get used to me."

Kelly stared straight ahead, using the paper as a shield. *And so will you.* He didn't voice the words. He didn't have to. But they were there between them. He sounded as if he were serving notice. But of what? Whatever it was, she wasn't going to touch that statement with the proverbial ten-foot pole. Giving the paper a defiant shake, she concentrated fiercely on the puzzle.

Jase watched her fingers tighten on the newspaper as she tacitly refused the challenge. His slow smile, had she seen it, would have infuriated her.

The silence gradually became a comfortable one, broken only by an occasional mutter from Jase as he read the directions and groped for a particular screw.

Kelly looked up. "What's a nine letter word for 'wretched?'"

Jase bolted one piece to another. "Miserable?"

"Ah."

Two hours, an almost-completed crossword puzzle, several cups of coffee and a constructed gas grill later, Kelly watched Jase collect his tools. "What are we going to do about the runaways?" she asked as they moved toward the door.

"Beats the hell out of me. Do you have any ideas?"

"Nope."

"The hotel said they left no forwarding address. And they made sure they didn't leave any clues on those tapes. 'South' could mean anywhere."

"What about Dick Tracy?"

"Who?"

"The guy you hired."

"Once I knew Dad had taken off on his own, I let him go."

"Oh. So now it's up to the two of us."

He nodded slowly. "Just the two of us."

The quiet statement brought her head up in surprise. It seemed to be saying more than should be possible with five short words.

"Jase."

The touch of his lips gently smothered whatever she intended to say. It also seemed to short-circuit her body and brain.

"Don't get too comfortable around me, Kelly," he warned huskily. "I'm not your brother." His hands rested on either side of her head, forming a cage, as she leaned against the door.

Definitely not a brother, she silently agreed, her eyes inching up his strong throat to his chin and stopping at his mouth.

"I'm not Mike. I'm not a casual date. I'm not someone you're going to get rid of with a friendly smile." His short statements were punctuated with soft kisses dropped on her upturned lips.

"Jase—" she began uncertainly.

"That's right," he agreed placidly, placing her hands on his shoulders and drawing her into his arms. "Jase. Whittaker." One of his large hands cupped the back of her unresisting head, the other settled on her hip, urging her closer, smoothing her curves to the hard planes of his body.

Jase Whittaker. The two words suddenly were synonymous with challenge, excitement and marauding masculinity. Definitely not a name or a man to be taken lightly.

Slowly, she drew back. At least an inch. Lowering her hands, which had inexplicably become clasped behind his neck, Kelly gave a tentative push against his chest. When it had no effect, she put some muscle behind it. "Jase, stop it. What are you trying to do?"

He drew in a sharp breath. "Call it whatever you want, honey. Making a statement. Staking a claim. Issuing a warning. It all means the same thing."

"Look," she pointed out with exaggerated calm, "we're supposed to be concentrating on finding my mother and your—" His words suddenly penetrated and her gaze swung up to clash with his. "What on earth are you talking about?"

"I want you, Kelly Lyndon. And before this is over, I intend to have you."

Her blue eyes flickered with sudden temper. Taking him by surprise, she ducked under his arms and moved out of reach. "I don't know who you think you are," she said, infuriated, "but I'm not going to let you walk into my life and turn it upside down!"

He stared at her for a moment with speculative eyes, then with a wolfish grin he turned and walked out the door.

Kelly stared after him, appalled. The gauntlet— however unintentionally thrown—had been accepted.

Chapter Five

*W*hat are you muttering about?'' Matt grinned down at the woman beside him, enjoying her total concentration. Her sleeveless yellow knit shirt was damp and softly molded her curves. She was flushed from the sun, her hair was a mess and he was crazy in love with her.

Her unblinking gaze remained on the shallow pan in her hands. ''I said that you disappoint me,'' she repeated blandly. ''I thought as a biggie in the business world, you would have a certain amount of perception, a bit of intuitive understanding—at least comprehend the difference between a simple statement and a request.''

The amusement gleaming in his turquoise eyes was replaced by a sudden flare of hunger for this woman. Shoving his hands in his back pockets, he told himself that he should be accustomed to it by now—but he wasn't. With an effort, he kept his voice light. "Must have been a shock to learn that we moguls sometimes have clay feet."

"It was, indeed," she promptly agreed. "But you seem like you'd be a fast learner."

"Try me."

Abby's hands faltered as she absorbed the unspoken plea—and promise—in his words, then resumed their rhythmic movement. Managing a brisk tone, she said, "Okay, listen up, Whittaker. If I comment that I've never been hang gliding, that's a statement, not an invitation to leap off a cliff. Got that?"

"Yep."

"So, when I said I had never panned for gold, I didn't expect to be packed into an ancient four-wheel drive, toted back into the hills by a whiskery prospector and dumped into a river of melted snow to look for nuggets." Vivid blue eyes, sparkling with laughter, rose to meet his.

"Poor baby," he mocked softly. "What've you got to show for all your work?"

She looked in disgust at a small mound of discarded sand and rock. "Diddly-squat," she admitted.

Matt reached for the pan she was patiently swirling. "Let me take over for a while."

Clutching the pan protectively in one arm, she batted at his hand. "No way. I'm staying here until I find something."

"Your feet will wrinkle in the water," he warned, grinning down at the stubborn woman. His stubborn woman.

"When you have gold fever," she explained airily, *"you put up with those little inconveniences."*

Matt straightened and stepped up on the sandy bank. *"Think an ice-cold beer will help the fever?"*

"Won't cure it, but it might ease the discomfort."

Abby's hands stilled as he walked away. Her hungry gaze followed his lithe frame. *He has the broad shoulders and trim hips of a much younger man,* she thought for the hundredth time. *A magnificent body. And, dear God, how I want that body next to mine!*

"Hmm," Mike mumbled, laying aside the small local newspaper. "What do you know. Someone found some gold at an old mining camp off Highway 49." He leaned back in the leather swivel chair, watching Kelly pace the length of the office. "Coyote, have you told him yet that I'm your cousin?"

"Ah..." Kelly looked up, apparently searching the ceiling for inspiration. Finding none, she slanted a quick glance at the large man and reluctantly shook her head.

"Why not?"

Perching on the corner of the desk, Kelly thought back, remembering how the fact that Mike was her cousin had been all the protection she'd ever needed. Now, she was absolutely, positively certain that the same information in the hands of one Jase Whittaker would have just the opposite effect. After vainly seeking a reasonable explanation, she shrugged and said, "It just seemed safer this way."

Mike's voice was dry. "For whom?"

Her tone matched his. "For me. You're big enough to take care of yourself."

"Size isn't everything," he muttered. "Coyote, your friend is working up a king-size hatred for me."

"That's never bothered you in the past," she said, intrigued.

"Considering the guys involved, there was no need. He's different."

She wiggled into a more comfortable position on the hard surface. "How?" she asked thoughtfully. She had reached the same conclusion the first time Jase had paced through the door, but she was curious how another male would explain the difference.

"When I played football," Mike began, "it never mattered what team I was up against. There was one quality that every man on that field had—killer instinct. It didn't matter how big the guy was, or how fast. If he didn't have that one quality, he didn't make it."

Kelly nodded encouragingly.

"Mine was well-honed, but it existed only on the field. The rest of the time, my size and reputation kept me from having to exert myself." He shrugged. "No one messes around with someone my size."

She nodded again, knowing the truth of that statement. "Go on."

"Whittaker," he continued gently, giving her thick braid a tug, "not only has it; he's never without it."

Kelly slid off the desk and resumed her restless pacing. Yes, she knew exactly what Mike meant. She was certain it was that quality—not nepotism—that enabled Jase to maintain his king-of-the-mountain position in the business world. The ability to spot an opening and use it to his advantage, she decided, was either bred in the bones or instilled in infancy. She wasn't sure which, but there was no denying that he had it, in spades.

"So he's got you worried?" she asked with a grin.

"Nope. The situation between us won't ever reach the hand-to-hand combat stage. Despite the fact that he ices over every time he sees me, I like him. And," his idle tone brought her head up, "I'd rather have him for a friend than an enemy. Ever find out exactly what he does?"

Kelly dropped down in the chair behind her desk. "Yeah. I asked Marge. She's the best snoop I know in the business world. Four years ago, Jase became a full partner in the Whittaker dynasty. In the past few months, Matt has been phasing out and Jase assuming more responsibility."

"What on earth are they doing in Fresno? You'd think they'd work out of New York or at least San Francisco."

"Clever, cousin," she applauded. "Their main office *is* in San Francisco. Matt grew up in this area and they kept the family home. Also, they're opening a branch in Fresno. Satisfied?"

"Yup." He leaned back, lacing his fingers behind his head. "So when are you going to let him off the hook?"

"What do you mean?" she asked, wide-eyed.

He tossed a pink eraser at her and smiled when she snagged it with an easy gesture. "Your act is slipping, Miss Innocence. You've let him think that I'm a big thing in your life."

"But, dahlink," she said with a heavy accent, "you are!"

"He's working up to something. You'd better tell him."

Her brows came together in a puzzled frown. "After all these years, why are you tossing me to the wolves now? Wolf," she amended quickly.

"Because you're getting to be an old lady," he teased. "You've got to learn how to handle these things, sooner or later. Besides, you can trust him." And he couldn't think of anyone *he* trusted more than that self-contained, competent man.

"And how do I casually drop it into a conversation after all this time?"

"You sound like you're talking about years. How long has it been?"

"Two weeks or so," she said gloomily. Two weeks, give or take a day, of Jase pacing around like a hungry dog sniffing at a juicy bone. And the only reason he'd kept that far away was because he thought Mike was firmly in the background.

"You can call me 'Cousin Mike' the next time he drops by," he suggested.

She looked at him in annoyance. "How subtle can you get? I know," she said, brightening after a thoughtful pause, "I'll just mention it as if I thought he knew. If he asks me, I'll say he must have forgotten because I introduced you that way. And you can back me up." She leaned forward, smiling with anticipation. "Okay?"

An affectionate, wicked grin creased his face. "Nope."

"Why not?" she asked, thoroughly incensed.

"Because you didn't."

"Since when have you gotten so scrupulous?"

"Since you started pussyfooting around the truth. Just tell him straight-out," he advised with a sigh, "and take your lumps."

"If I do that, how am I going to handle him when we're running around looking for Mom?" she asked. "You were my big gun held in reserve."

"You'll manage," he said without sympathy. "You always do. By the way, what's the latest on the runaways?"

"Don't ask," she groaned. "They're driving me nuts! We've been out on three false alarms and every day I find a message on my answering machine. I learn that the weather's fine, Mom's fine, and Matt's fine. Aside from that, it's one big zip. Then, when Jase gets home, he finds exactly the same message, only in Matt's voice."

"Well, isn't that what's important? To know that they're safe and well?"

"Yeah," she mumbled uncertainly, "I guess so."

"Then why are you hellbent on finding Aunt Abby and dragging her home?"

His question hung in the air between them for a moment. She sighed inwardly, knowing it wouldn't be easy to explain. Guilt rarely was.

Kelly began slowly, carefully selecting her words. "I've nagged Mom for so long about being in a rut, I guess I need to know that what she's doing is because she wants to do it and not because I've driven her to it." She finished in a rush and watched Mike to see if he understood.

He understood all right, and he wasn't impressed with her rationale. "Come on, Kelly. She's ignored you all these years, so what makes you think that she'd turn her life upside down because you ran through the lecture one more time? Face it, babe, she's with Matt because she wants to be."

"Maybe," she said grudgingly. "But I'm sticking to Jase like glue, because when he finds them, I'm worried about what he'll say. He thinks Mom is some...some...*vamp* who's got her claws into a rich man and—"

"Vamp?" He looked down at her determined face and bit back a grin. "I'm going to take a good look at that lady when she gets back. First I hear she's a banquet, then she's giving people palpitations and hot flashes, now a vamp?"

"It's not funny, Mike." Kelly glared up into amused hazel eyes. "I won't have her hurt."

Mike hauled her into his arms and planted a kiss on the top of her head. "I have a feeling that if Jase is fool enough to say what he's thinking when he finally sees them—and mind you, babe, he's no fool—Matt Whittaker is all the protection that she's going to need."

Kelly wrapped her arms around his waist and rested her head on his chest. "I wish I were as sure as you are," she said with a sigh.

It was unfortunate, she thought later—when she was once again capable of coherent thought—that Jase chose that particular moment to walk through the doorway. At the sound of his glacial voice, Mike's arm instinctively tightened just as she tried to jerk away. They looked like illicit lovers caught by an outraged husband, she decided. *Sneaky*, illicit lovers.

"Kelly." Jase nodded a cool greeting, watching with enigmatic eyes as she pulled herself from Mike's embrace. "Mike," he acknowledged, in a voice that, other than being tinged with frost, gave nothing away.

He was clad in one of his sexy suits again, Kelly noted absently. This time it was light gray. By all rights, she thought, the color shouldn't have suited him, but it deepened his tan and did fantastic things to his eyes.

Ignoring Mike, he asked, "Ready for another wild goose chase?"

She nodded. "Now? Where?"

"Not too far. Up 49 a bit. A tourist place near one of the old mining camps. Seems an attractive blond woman, who prefers to remain anonymous, found a couple of good-sized nuggets. It has possibilities."

Mike gave a helpless crack of laughter. "You mean Aunt Abby's started another gold rush?"

"Mike!" Kelly darted apprehensive eyes at Jase.

His narrow-eyed gaze was centered on the younger man. "Aunt?" he asked sharply.

Ignoring him, Mike reeled Kelly back in and placed a smacking kiss on her forehead. "Babe," he said, grinning, "it sounds like your mom is having the time of her life. Sure you want to find her and spoil it all?"

Eyeing them speculatively, Jase repeated, "Aunt?"

With Mike's warm hand at her waist for moral support, Kelly turned and gave wide-eyed innocence her best shot. "Didn't I tell you that Mike was my cousin?"

"No," Jase said dryly, "you didn't."

"Well, I'll be darned," she mumbled, smiling tentatively at him then turning to cast a quelling glance at Mike as she felt a tremor of amusement run through him. "I did remember to tell you that he was my partner, didn't I?'' she asked, glancing back at Jase. Don't push it, she advised herself. If you're smart, you'll keep your mouth shut and concentrate on separating the two of them.

Jase calmly stepped forward and removed her from Mike's arms. His voice was, if possible, even dryer. "You made that quite clear," he assured her.

"Oh, good." She looked up with a brilliant smile.

He stared down at her for a moment. "Woman," he said evenly, "I hope you don't ever play strip poker. You don't bluff worth a damn and I'd sure hate to see you walking around without a stitch on. In public, that is." He bent his head and dropped a hard kiss on her soft, full lips.

Looking across her head at the large, smiling man, he said, "I'll be back to talk to you."

"Do that," Mike said amicably. "I'll have a cold beer ready."

Jase turned the key and opened the door of the most gorgeous Victorian house Kelly had ever seen. He flipped on the lights in the entryway and stood back, waiting for her to enter.

Kelly was a sucker for old houses. Ignoring the little voice inside her that chattered frantically of wily spiders and gullible flies, she stepped inside and tried to see it all at once. While the outside had been beautifully restored, polished and painted until it equalled any of San Francisco's Painted Ladies, the inside was an architectural dream. Her encompassing glance took in the high ceilings, large rooms with creamy walls, and gold drapes. Mellow wood tones struck an inviting note, and furniture in shades of cinnamon, beige and chocolate completed the effect.

It was not a blatantly masculine house, she noted with surprise. Somehow, she had expected Jase's home to be cooler, a bit formal and distant. The gracious warmth it generated left her feeling a bit off balance.

Shedding his coat and tie as he walked over to a fruitwood sideboard, Jase asked, "Brandy?"

Kelly dropped down on a plump sofa and looked through to the dining room, admiring the brass and crystal chandelier. Shaking her head, she said, "Can't stand the stuff."

"Wine?"

"Please. Not too dry."

He handed her the glass and sat down next to her. Leaning back, he stared at the pale amber wine. "Another fiasco," he said grimly, thinking of the old man who had quietly admitted Matt and Abby had been in his camp and stubbornly claimed ignorance of their present location.

"You have to admit it was interesting, though," she said thoughtfully. With a sudden giggle, she asked, "Will you ever forget the expression on his face when he told us that Mom left him the gold? He couldn't believe that anyone would pan just for the fun of it. But I feel kind of sorry for him."

As Jase's brows lifted in curiosity, she nodded. "I do. He may be a few nuggets ahead, but he's going to have weekend prospectors crawling all over that pretty little valley for months to come."

Nodding absently in agreement, Jase asked, "Do you suppose they're deliberately trying to make fools of us?"

At the quietly asked question, she turned and examined his expression. "No," she said thoughtfully, "I don't think that ever entered their minds. I have a feeling that they're just trying to buy some time—uninterrupted, private time. They probably have no idea that we're running around like crazy people trying to find them."

With a shock, she realized that Abby's breezy messages had finally penetrated, removed her niggling sense of guilt. No—transferred it, she amended silently. She no longer insisted on assuming responsibility for Abby's disappearance, but she was becoming increasingly uncomfortable with the idea of playing detective. Her enthusiasm was definitely on the wane; the chase was no longer fun or exciting. She quailed at the thought of what the older couple would have to say about it. Probably something like "unwarranted interference," just for starters.

"Mike said," she began, only to find the words dwindling away as Jase slanted a wry look at her.

"Ah, yes. Mike."

Damning her habit of speaking before thinking, Kelly gave a mental groan. Oh, well, what the hell. No sense in stretching out the agony, she decided. The subject was about as volatile as nitroglycerin bouncing in a truck bed on a rain-rutted road. If the look on Jase's face was any indication, he had a few choice words to say about the matter and she had a sinking feeling that he was going to say them, come hell or high water. Might as well let him get it out of his system.

With that in mind, she asked, "Are you mad about this cousin thing?"

Jase draped his arm across her shoulders and nudged her closer, until her head rested in the hollow of his shoulder. Mad? Good God! Anger was the last thing on his mind. Dizzy with relief was closer to the truth. She obviously had no idea how much time during the past two weeks—when he should have been concentrating on a myriad of other things—he had spent devising plans to sever her relationship with one Michael Trent.

There were any number of things he could have done, but he'd restrained himself because he liked the other man—or would have, if he hadn't believed that Trent was just a stone's throw away from becoming Kelly's lover. And Jase had decided right from the beginning that he would be the only man in Kelly Lyndon's bed.

Kelly did not foster placid feelings within him, Jase realized. In fact, for a man who was considered by some to be restrained and dispassionate, he'd had to cope with a number of surprisingly potent emotions in the past couple of weeks. She amused him, irritated him beyond measure, entertained him with her rather naive reflections on human nature, and most of all, elicited a savage hunger within him that only her sweet body could satisfy.

He looked down on her unsuspecting head. If the way she relaxed in his arms was any measure of her innocence, Trent had been one hell of a watchdog. He wondered if she had any idea how her soft warmth stirred the fires within him. Probably not, or she'd be bolting out the door. Since the night at her house when they'd both issued and accepted a challenge, she had been understandably wary of him. But tonight, either the long drive or the wine at dinner had lowered her defenses. And that's how he wanted her, he realized with surprise. Not fighting him, not issuing challenges, not patting him with friendly affection, but allowing her body to lean into his, filling his arms with womanly softness.

An elbow in his ribs brought him back to the present. "You're either very mad," she said, her voice almost whimsical, "or comatose."

Forcing himself to relax, stretching his long body out next to hers, he said, "Neither." Watch it, he warned himself. One wrong word and it'll be like setting a match to dynamite. "It did clear up a minor problem, though."

"What?" She turned slightly, her cheek brushing his shoulder as she stared up at him.

His lashes lowered over gleaming eyes and his voice matched the casual sprawl of his body. "Why you treated Mike like a brother, and why he permitted it."

Kelly chuckled lazily. "He almost is. We grew up together and he watched over me like a mother hen."

"Some hen," he observed, delicately tracing her jawline with his thumb. She shivered and became instantly still. Alert to her sudden tension, Jase let his hand slide down her arm to ensnare her fingers. He wasn't ready to be deprived of her warmth.

To Kelly's finely tuned senses, a certain tension invaded the room, replacing her sense of well-being. And it definitely emanated from the man beside her. If she was ever going to heed her inner voice, she decided, the time was now.

"Well," she said with forced briskness, preparing to rise, "we've got that settled. As long as you understand that I didn't lie to you." Getting up from the sofa, she found, although absolutely imperative, was not going to be easy. Somehow, without exerting any pressure at all, Jase seemed to have her linked securely to his side. On one side, his fingers were laced through hers. On the other, they slowly caressed the intricacies of her thick braid. She gave an inward sigh of relief. At least both his hands were occupied in a fairly innocent occupation. That was a blessing of no small order. The blasted man had a knack for finding subtle nerve endings that she didn't even know existed. And he knew exactly how she responded when he touched them. How could he not, she wondered gloomily, when her body seemed hell-bent on betrayal?

Jase glanced down at her. "You don't call that a lie?"

"Of course not!" she assured him. "I simply hadn't gotten around to mentioning it."

He nodded, clearly fascinated with her logic. "Omissions aren't lies?" he persevered.

"Absolutely not. For instance. I haven't told you that I wore braces for two years. Is that a lie?"

"Nope."

"Or that I played first base on a softball team. Is that a lie?"

"Not at all."

He seemed to be more interested in undoing her braid than following the conversation, Kelly noted. Sensing that victory was within her grasp, she added, "So, tell me what the difference is." Obviously pleased with her defense, she stared up at him.

Using both hands to finish unraveling her braid, Jase didn't answer for a moment. His eyes glinted in pure, masculine satisfaction as the mass of sun-streaked hair tumbled down to the center of her back.

"Would you say that motivation has some bearing on the question?" he asked gently.

Blinking, she repeated the word as if she had never run into it before.

He nodded. "You might have gotten around to mentioning braces and baseball someday, but you were making damn sure I didn't learn that Mike was your cousin. Why was that so important, Kelly?"

Spiders, Kelly remembered in disgust, not only extended invitations to stupid flies, they also spun webs in which to trap them. So much for logic.

"What were you afraid of?" His voice was soft, almost hypnotic.

Just how dumb did he think she was? He already had the advantage of experience. Apparently, lots of it. Did he think she was going to tell him that in the face of his determined pursuit, her chance of survival was less than a snowball's in Death Valley?

She flashed him a brilliant smile. "Not afraid, Jase," she corrected, "just careful."

"Honey," his head lowered and his mouth brushed softly over hers, "I warned you earlier about bluffing."

Chapter Six

*M*att shifted his hips and waited patiently until Abby looked up with a smile. For a man who had spent his life making things happen, learning patience was not an easy task. But he had discovered early in life that rewards usually matched or exceeded the effort expended in achieving a goal. Abby was more than he had ever dreamed of having. Patience was a small price to pay.

He patted the space beside him on the chaise. "You look lonely over there," he said, admiring the picture she made in white cotton shorts and a matching sleeveless top with a round, scooped neck. "Come and join me."

"I thought you'd never ask," she admitted with the naturalness that never failed to surprise him. With a quick, neat movement, she stretched out beside him. "Ah, this is . . ." Her words broke off on a gasp as his *hand trailed up her thigh and stopped, shaping the soft curve of her abdomen. "Nice," she finished faintly, meeting the intent expression in his eyes.*

Changing the subject abruptly, she looked around at the expanse of green lawn bordering the gracious old house. "This inn is wonderful, isn't it?"

"Umm," he agreed lazily. "It would be perfect for a honeymoon." Inhaling deeply, he forced himself to ignore her sudden tension.

Abby swallowed dryly. He certainly didn't beat around the bush. But then, that was something she had learned within two minutes after meeting him. An indecisive, dithering man wouldn't have asked, after one encompassing glance at her staid dress and controlled hairstyle, "Are we going to a board meeting or a dance?" A less determined man would never have coerced her, however gently, into admitting that she had in her possession a fascinating blue dress and agreeing to let her hair down—both literally and figuratively. And any other man certainly wouldn't have convinced her, within the span of five hours, to run away with him.

"Matt," she said after a long pause. "It's been such a short time. I want you to be sure."

"I am." His tone left no room for doubt. "We're only waiting for you to decide."

Shifting his weight, Matt rested on his elbow, leaning over her. For once, a smile did not lighten his expression. "And, Abby," he warned gently, "if you say yes, be very sure you mean it, because once I know that you're mine, I'll never let you go."

Two days later, on her hands and knees in her backyard, trying to lure Annie out of the bushes and into a large tub of water, Kelly was still considering the merits of bluffing. She really wasn't any good at it, she cheerfully admitted to herself; probably never would be. But then, if she were more proficient, she would have missed out on the most shattering kiss of her life. Excellence is not always its own reward, she decided with a grin.

Grabbing Annie and easing her into the water, Kelly thought about that kiss. There are kisses, and then there are *kisses*, she decided. Until just recently, hers had all fallen into the first category. Most of them were interesting, pleasantly exciting, and not terribly demanding. Jase's was definitely the second type. In fact, she had the feeling that he had just introduced her to a whole new world of emotional communication.

"Don't look so pathetic," she advised the dog. "It won't work. We'll be through here in a couple of minutes." Lathering shampoo into Annie's soaking coat, she pondered. If the sexual tension that surrounded Jase at times was a typical male characteristic, how on earth had she escaped running into it somewhere along the way? After all, she was almost twenty-five and, despite the fact that she lived in a small town, she had met her fair share of men. And while this part of the country was not exactly a seething bed of intrigue and affairs, it certainly wasn't provincial. In fact, thanks to its proximity to Yosemite, it hosted visitors from all over the world.

Absently rinsing Annie off with the hose, she smiled reminiscently, thinking of the man from France she had dated several times. His kisses were . . . well, practised. She tilted her head, consideringly. They hadn't been bad though, not bad at all. But something had been lacking. There was never a feeling, as with Jase, of hunger lying in wait, of passion barely controlled. As a matter of fact, now that she thought about it, she had the feeling that each time René had kissed her, he kept one eye open watching out for Mike.

It was demoralizing to think that while she'd spent the latter years of her life waiting for kisses that produced fireworks and earthquakes, Mike had spent those same years diverting the type of man who could provide them. Her cousin had a lot to answer for, she decided, wrapping Annie's wiggling form in a large towel to absorb most of the moisture. Did he realize exactly what he had deprived her of? Very likely, her inner voice answered dryly.

Fortunately for her, he had fallen down on the job where Jase was concerned. But she had the feeling that if he knew how easily Jase had turned her into his arms the other night, he'd be right back on the job. Maybe Mike should have let one or two of the advanced group sneak through a few years ago, she thought with a frown. Then she might have some idea of how to cope with a man like Jase. Because he was definitely out of her league.

Jase had been in no hurry that night. After brushing her lips with his, he had taken his time. He'd just held back, waiting. Like an eagle soaring overhead, watching for a rabbit to break and run, he'd waited for her to look up at him. And, dammit, she had! After a pause that seemed to last for hours, she couldn't stand the suspense any longer. Once she raised her chin, he

...be tempted!

**See inside for special
4 FREE BOOKS offer**

Silhouette Romance ®

Discover deliciously different Romance with 4 Free Novels from

Silhouette Romance®

...be enchanted!

As a Silhouette home subscriber, the enchantment begins with Debbie Macomber's CHRISTMAS MASQUERADE, the story of Jo Marie, in love with another woman's fiancé...Arlene James' NOW OR NEVER, when a man and woman live under the same roof, just one touch can lead them anywhere...Emilie Richards' GILDING THE LILY, which takes you into the heart of a woman who has always held back—until now...and Rita Rainville's WRITTEN ON THE WIND, the story of a beautiful woman on the trail of a corporate spy—and a new romance?

...be our guest!

These exciting, love-filled, full-length novels are yours *absolutely FREE along with your Folding Umbrella and Mystery Gift...a present from us to you. They're yours to keep no matter what you decide.

...be delighted!

After you receive your 4 FREE books, we'll send you 6 more Silhouette Romance novels each and every month to examine FREE for 15 days. If you decide to keep them, pay just $11.70—with no additional charges for home delivery! If you aren't completely delighted, just drop us a note and we'll cancel your subscription, no questions asked. **EXTRA BONUS:** You'll also receive the Silhouette Books Newsletter FREE with each book shipment. Every issue is filled with interviews, news about upcoming books, recipes from your favorite authors, and more.

To get your 4 FREE novels, Folding Umbrella, and Mystery Gift, just fill out and mail the attached order card. Remember, the first 4 novels and both gifts are yours to keep. Are you ready to be tempted?

Mail this card today for

4 FREE BOOKS
(a $7.80 value)
this Folding Umbrella and
a Mystery Gift *ALL FREE!*

Clip and mail this postpaid card today! 2

Silhouette Romance ®

Silhouette Books, 120 Brighton Rd., P.O. Box 5084, Clifton, NJ 07015-9956

☐ **YES!** Please send me my four Silhouette Romance novels along with my FREE Folding Umbrella and Mystery Gift, as explained in the attached insert. I understand that I am under no obligation to purchase any books.

NAME _____

(please print)

ADDRESS _____

CITY _____ STATE _____ ZIP _____

CAR086

had ignored her glare and the heated words she was preparing. His lips pressed down on hers and *bingo*. There were fireworks and even a bit of "The Hallelujah Chorus." Afterward, she'd been breathless, her brain swirling with vertigo, much as she imagined the feeling would be if one were lucky enough to survive being swept up in a tsunami.

Exciting as it had been, it was obvious that Jase shouldn't be allowed to walk around freely on the streets. He was clearly a man to be avoided—unless you liked playing with fire. Brushing the groaning dog with the towel, she wondered idly how a man evolved from an infant into a sexy menace. Was it environment, information passed from father to son, or something genetic? Whatever it was, she realized with a shock, if Jase was a true reflection of Matt, and if her mother had been exposed to the same potent brand of masculinity she had been coping with, *and* if her mother was as intrigued as she was, then Abby was not being restrained against her will. She knew exactly what she was doing!

Stunned by that bit of deductive reasoning, Kelly slid from her knees to sit on the grass. Engrossed in her own startling thoughts, she didn't even notice Annie break loose and promptly roll in the grass to remove the faint fragrance of the shampoo. It wasn't until the small dog trotted back to settle at her side, growling deep in her throat, that Kelly looked up.

Speak of the devil, she thought wryly as she spotted Jase and a beautifully formed German shepherd walking toward her. Jase was wearing jeans and the Western-style shirt and gleaming boots he seemed to favor in his leisure time.

"Hi, cowboy," she said, managing to talk despite her sudden breathlessness. *My God, he's absolutely gorgeous,* she decided, wondering how she had ever thought he was too grim, too harsh. Hard on the heels of that biased opinion came the realization that he was nothing but a ten-gallon hat full of trouble. He was a man who spoke a lot about wanting and having, staking claims and issuing warnings, and a big zip about loving and commitment. He wasn't exactly the type who encouraged a woman to think about home, hearth, and jars of baby food.

Jase sat down tailor-fashion, facing her. "Hi. I thought our dogs should get acquainted."

Kelly blinked in surprise. "Why?"

"When two people are developing a relationship, it—"

"Is that what we're doing?"

"Yes. It stands to reason—"

"That sounds more serious than saying we've known each other for a couple of weeks."

"It is. It stands to reason that their dogs—"

"Some relationships never get off the ground," she pointed out objectively.

"—should have a chance to form their own relationship," he finished grimly. "Ours will," he added. "You can bet on that." He stretched out full-length on the grass, propping himself up on one elbow.

"At times, it's damned hard holding a conversation with you that makes sense," he complained mildly.

Kelly unfolded her legs, stretching them before her. Draping her arms around her slightly bent knees, she said, "I understood every word you said. What's your dog's name?"

"Shep."

A delighted gurgle of laughter escaped her. "I don't believe it. Nobody, absolutely nobody, names a shepherd 'Shep' anymore."

His voice was absent as he ran a finger along the gentle curve of her leg from ankle to knee. "*I* do. He doesn't seem to care. What about Annie?"

"What about her?" she asked vaguely. "Oh, Annie!" she said, trying to capture Jase's hand. "There's a perfectly logical reason for her name." She moved her legs an inch or so to the right. "Mike found her and—"

Jase groaned. "Don't tell me. You called her Annie because she was an orphan."

Kelly regarded him with pleased surprise. "That's right."

A reluctant grin creased his face. "It scares the hell out of me when I realize that I'm beginning to understand the way you think."

"You should be so lucky," she retorted. The sound of a low growl brought her head around. Shep stood looking down at Annie with a patently bored expression on his face, while the small dog walked around him, stiff-legged with antagonism. "I think there's something wrong with your master plan," Kelly pointed out. "They aren't exactly oozing with friendship."

"Give them time," Jase said carelessly. "Good relationships sometimes take a little longer to gel."

Her quick glance was suspicious. "Are you trying to tell me something?" she demanded.

"Wouldn't dream of it," he denied, surging to his feet and reaching for her hand. "Come on, let's go."

"Where?"

"A picnic."

"Wait a minute, Jase. Polite men do not drop in unexpectedly and drag people off to picnics without first asking if those people have something else planned." By the time she finished, she was digging her bare heels into the ground to slow him down.

He stopped and stared down at her. "Do you have anything planned?"

"No," she reluctantly admitted, silently cursing her honesty and inability to invent convenient excuses. It wasn't smart to spend any more time with him than necessary. And even that amount was dangerous. "No, I don't," she repeated slowly, "but—"

"Good," he interrupted, walking her briskly upstairs to the deck. "Get your shoes, bathing suit and whatever else you need for a picnic. I'll collect the dogs."

That wasn't going to be a difficult task, she thought, considering that they were clambering up the steps right behind the two of them.

"We're taking them?" she asked.

Jase nodded, smiling with satisfaction. But not at the question. They both knew that she had just agreed to go. And they both knew that she was a bit apprehensive about her decision. Furthermore, she realized, glaring at his pleased look, they both knew that she wouldn't admit it for the world.

"I thought you said we were going on a picnic?"

"That's right." Jase nodded in agreement, turning the jeep into his driveway. "Where else can we let the dogs run loose?" He reached behind him and opened the back door. Shep politely remained seated and let Annie leap out. She hit the ground running and disappeared around the corner of the house.

He walked around and opened Kelly's door, wondering if she would move as impetuously as her dog. He had noticed a number of similarities between the two. Both were honey-colored, neither one seemed to know when it was sensible to back down before a larger and tougher opponent, and both were quite vocal. But today, he noted as Kelly slowly swung her legs out, things were different. The lady was being cautious for once in her life.

He draped an arm around her shoulders and led her around the corner of the house.

It was a huge yard with an enormous pool. He obviously did some serious swimming out here, she thought, eyeing the pool with a practised glance. Laps, she decided. He probably comes out here every day, propelling himself from one end to the other with those muscular arms. He'd go back and forth until his disciplined mind told his disciplined body that he'd had enough.

Kicking off her shoes, she walked to the edge of the pool and dipped one foot in the water. Turning with a quick smile, she said, "It's heaven! Where can I change?"

Jase nodded to a dressing room at the far end and watched until the door closed behind her. Then he smiled. He took great pleasure in her vivid coloring, her spontaneity. She reminded him of a butterfly, flitting here and there, curious, artlessly investigating the world at large. His lips curved in another smile. A picture flashed into his mind of wings fluttering over his extended palm. When they stilled and the fragile butterfly delicately touched his hand, it would be a simple task to form a protective cage around it.

Kelly approached the pool at a dead run and hit the water curled up in a cannonball. When she surfaced, Jase was examining the spreading wet spots on his clothes. He just might have to temper that spontaneity a bit, he decided, as he turned toward the dressing room.

When he emerged, Kelly was on the grass delivering a lecture. Shep looked bored and Annie was visibly sulking.

Jase balanced easily on the edge of the pool. "Trouble?"

"Annie seems to think that she's King Kong. She's trying to hassle Shep. If you know what's good for you," she advised the small dog, "you'll knock it off. He's more than twice your size."

Kelly turned, her eyes widening as she took in the sight of Jase without clothes. Almost without. That tiny excuse of a suit left an awful lot uncovered.

Taking a deep breath, she walked slowly past Jase, trying to ignore the impact of his wide shoulders, broad chest and flat stomach. She wouldn't give him the satisfaction of staring at the crisp mat of hair that narrowed and disappeared beneath the waist of the slim racing trunks. Suddenly, before she talked herself out of it, she whirled, placed a hand on his chest and pushed. He made a magnificent splash.

Jase surged to the surface and shook the hair out of his eyes. A gleam lightened his aquamarine gaze. Yes. The dog did indeed take after her mistress.

"Kelly, sometimes you've got more courage than good sense," he commented evenly.

"I know." She stood at the edge of the pool, trim in her ice-blue, fairly conservative bikini. Her solemn voice was in direct contrast to her laughing eyes. "I've got to work on that."

"I'll help you," he offered, calmly reaching for her.

Catching Kelly was not as easy as it looked. She let out a shriek, darted to the other end of the pool and jumped in.

For five minutes, she used the water to her advantage, evading him. He was strong, but she was as agile as an eel. Finally, she miscalculated.

Jase's hand settled around her ankle and pulled her to him. She fought every inch of the way as he towed her to the shallow end, lifted her and draped her over his shoulder.

"Jase!" she gasped amid laughter. "Let me go." Her groping hand found his thick pelt of hair and tugged.

A large hand landed on her softly rounded bottom in retaliation.

"You're no gentleman!"

"You're right."

"Are you going to let me down?"

"Nope."

"This is your last chance," she warned.

"Do your worst," he said with a grin.

"Annie! Help me! Come and bite this chauvanistic, muscle-bound—"

"Damn it!"

"What happened?"

"She bit me!"

"*What?*"

"She bit me."

"I don't believe it."

"Why not?" he asked, setting her on her feet. "You told her to."

"Well, I certainly didn't think she would. Are you sure? She doesn't even know what the command means."

Jase held up an ankle for her inspection.

Kelly examined the teeth marks and then beamed down at the dog. "What a bright baby."

"Don't you dare praise her for that."

"But she came to my rescue," she explained cautiously. "I have to let her know that she did the right thing. What if you had been a burglar or something? She really did a good job," Kelly insisted, turning her eyes away from the marks on his leg.

For once, Jase had nothing to say. Kelly glanced back up at him to find a fascinated expression on his face. "Why are you looking at me like that?"

"Like what?"

"Like I'm about to grow another head. You do that frequently," she told him.

"Is that the kind of logic you use on the dogs at the kennel?"

"Fortunately for all concerned," she admitted cheerfully, "Mike is the expert on dogs. I just follow orders where they're concerned. I—" she tapped a spot above her bikini top that drew his eyes to her pert breasts "—am the brains behind the business."

The gaze that was thoroughly inspecting the bikini lifted to her face. She was serious, he realized, examining her serenely confident expression. She was really serious.

"I'll get the food," he said, turning to the house. "And you," he called over his shoulder, "explain to that mutt that I'm a friend."

"Then try acting like one," she muttered to his disappearing back. In her opinion, a friend was someone you could talk with, laugh with, be comfortable with. Not someone who overflowed with masculine hormones, who seemed ready to pounce at the slightest provocation.

Some of the tension sparking between them dissipated during lunch. His hormones became nicely insulated, she decided, as he ate a ham sandwich; and after a glass of chilled white wine, his pouncing tendencies seemed to diminish.

"Tell me about your partnership." The abrupt question brought her head up.

Kelly placed her elbows on the glass tabletop and stared at him thoughtfully. "When we were in our teens we made our plans. We both loved animals and knew we could make a go of it. As time passed, I discovered I had an affinity for financial matters. About the same time, Mike informed me that while I loved dogs to distraction, I was awful when it came to disciplining them."

Amused blue-green eyes looked back at her. "I can see that you agree," she sighed.

"So what did you do?"

"I majored in business administration and did very well. Mike and I make a good team."

"That's obvious. It looks like your business is flourishing." He could afford to be generous now that Trent no longer loomed as a threat.

"It is. We'll soon be ready to enlarge the facilities." She lifted her wineglass and swallowed. "What about you?"

"My business? It's exacting, but I like the work and I'm good at what I do."

Talk about a master of understatement! Kelly had a fair idea of the scope of his business dealings. He wasn't minimizing them, she realized, he had just learned to deal with them. And she had the feeling that he wasn't being modest. He was probably very good indeed!

Annie sat close to Kelly's chair and dropped a damp ball at her feet.

Jase leaned over to collect it and tossed it across the yard. "I brought you a friend to play with," he informed the dog. "Kelly's going to play with me."

"Play what?" she asked with suspicion.

His brows rose in mock surprise. "Ball," he said blandly. "What else?"

He was entirely too innocent, she decided after a quick glance.

"You can catch a ball, can't you?"

"With a football player in the family, there's no way that I couldn't catch one," she assured him.

"Can you throw one?"

"Try me."

He stood up, supported his hands on the sides of the table and leaned forward, a whisper away from her lips. "I can't wait," he muttered, stopping her breath with a slow, thorough kiss.

Kelly placed her hands on his chest. Trying to ignore the tantalizing touch of the crisp, dark hair beneath her fingers, she applied pressure. Slowly, he moved back. His reluctance was obvious. His hunger was also obvious, but he still had it under control, she noted with relief.

Touching his tongue to his lips, he said, "You taste like wine."

"So do you." She cleared her throat and kept her voice as matter-of-fact as possible. "I'll change out of my suit while you get the ball." At his slow nod, she breathed a sigh of relief.

This is not called running, she told herself bracingly, as she turned and walked away. The hell it isn't! her inner voice commented dryly.

Back in her pale-yellow shorts and top, she decided that quelling her inner voice was easier than facing Jase again. He waited by the pool, casually tossing the football into the air. His skimpy suit, she noted with relief, had been shed in favor of cutoff jeans. When he looked up, it was obvious that some vestige of electricity remained, still sparking between them.

Coming to a halt a safe distance away, she called, "Ready!"

Jase threw the ball with an ease that Kelly envied. She caught it without difficulty and returned it. She wasn't as proficient as he was, of course, but at least it didn't wobble all over, she thought with satisfaction.

Jase carefully geared the speed of the ball to her smaller stature. She appreciated the gesture, but in her opinion it made the game a bit slow.

The next time he threw it, she changed the game plan. Cupping the ball against her body with one arm, she zigzagged across the lawn around imaginary obstacles and ran past him. Bouncing the ball on the ground in the tradition of winners, she shouted, "Touchdown!" Without looking at Jase, she picked up the ball and returned to her original position, calling over her shoulder, "One-zip."

When Jase caught the ball he exploded into action. He looked like a rampaging bull, she thought in panic, as he headed straight for her. Holding her ground just long enough to touch his arm, she leaped out of the way.

Not fast enough, she decided an instant later. Jase slowed down long enough to pick her up and cross an imaginary line. Setting her on her feet, he cupped her head with a large hand and kissed her, slowly wrapping his other arm around her, drawing her close. When he straightened, he was breathing fast. His eyes met hers. "One up."

Kelly narrowed her eyes and watched him walk away. In her opinion, he looked entirely too pleased with himself. A moment later, she plucked the ball out of the air and took off like a rocket. This time Jase was ready for her. Kelly did what any reasonable person would do: she called for reinforcements. "Annie! Annie! Go get him!"

Annie, she noted, had apparently decided that Jase wasn't so bad. She went for him all right. She leaped into his arms and covered his face with wet, canine kisses. In the confusion, Kelly breezed past them. "Two-one," she chortled.

Jase finally emptied his arms of the dog and wiped his face clean of kisses.

"You cheated."

Kelly nodded complacently. "I know. I learned a long time ago that I never win if I play by the rules."

"I break the rules every now and then myself," Jase commented, strolling over to her.

Edging nervously away, Kelly muttered, "Do you, now?"

"Uh-hmm."

Kelly broke and ran in the direction of the back gate. Before she reached it, Jase tackled her, gently bringing her down on the thick grass. He caught her in his arms, taking the brunt of the fall, then rolled over until she was on her back and he was straddling her.

Not one to take defeat well, Kelly started yelling. "Help! Annie, get me help! Call the National Guard! Call the police!"

With shocking suddenness, a firm, baritone voice came from over Jase's shoulder, somewhere near the gate. "Yes, ma'am. What can we do for you?"

Moving warily, Jase rose and extended a hand to help Kelly up. Leaning against him, within the protective curve of his arm, she looked at the two men standing by the ornamental gate. My God, was her shocked thought, it's like something out of a TV detective show. The two men, conventionally clad in slacks and sport coats, had "police" written all over them.

Chapter Seven

Abby laced her fingers through Matt's until their palms touched. They stood on the uneven sidewalk of the old gold-rush town. "What do you want to do today?"

With satisfying promptness, Matt replied, "Go back to the inn and make love to you."

Her brows rose as she tried not to grin. "All day?"

"For starters."

"Don't I have anything to say about it?"

"Sure. You get to choose the place. Your room or mine."

Abby laughed softly. "Speaking of our rooms, I heard the women in the office trying to figure out why we have two."

Matt slanted a humorous look at her. "Sometimes I have trouble with that one myself." His fingers tightened on hers. "I heard them, too. They called it extravagant."

"Isn't it fortunate that you're so rich you can indulge my every whim?"

Matt looked down at her with amused interest. "Who told you that?"

"You did," she said with composure. "When you were trying to talk me into running away with you."

"Did I really say that?" he asked in disbelief. "That sounds just a tad pompous."

She gave a pleasant nod. "I thought so, too. That's one of the reasons I decided to come."

He tilted his head questioningly. "You have a thing for pompous men?"

"Far from it. But I got the impression that you were restraining some pretty strong emotions. In fact, by the time you finished your little speech, all the feelings had been wrung out of the words. Everything sounded pretty stilted. You definitely weren't the articulate man I had spent the evening with."

He looked down at the tender smile curving her lips, and frowned. "So you came with me because you felt sorry for me? I don't need or want your pity, Abby."

She nodded approvingly. "Good. Because you're not a man who would ever get it."

"Then why did you come?"

"Two reasons. One was that I had to know why you seemed almost..."

"What?"

"I'm not sure. Almost frantic."

He nodded grimly. "An appropriate word. I couldn't believe my eyes when you opened the door. I

*needed you, and you needed time. By the end of the
evening I was desperate."*

*He broke the thoughtful silence, asking finally,
"What was the second reason?"*

*Looking down, he was surprised to see color flood-
ing her face. "Abby?" Stopping the middle of the
walk, Matt brought her to a halt beside him.*

*Knowing that the stubborn man would make tour-
ists walk around them until he received an answer, she
blurted, "It was your eyes. They said everything that
your awful little speech didn't. They made me
feel . . . special, desirable. And—" Her voice cracked.*

Matt's low voice was urgent. "And what, Abby?"

*"In all my life, no one has ever wanted me so des-
perately."*

"Who the hell are you, and what do you want?"

Kelly had heard varied inflections in Jase's voice
and witnessed many of his mood shifts over the past
few weeks. She had seen him taken aback, cool, puzzled, determined and, when around Mike, subtly
emanating a threat in a purely masculine way. She had
heard neither the intimidating lash of authority nor
experienced his aura of genuine, physical menace.
Everything about him indicated that the two intrud-
ers had better come up with an immediate, satisfactory explanation—or else.

The two men dug into their breast pockets and
withdrew slim wallets. They flipped them open to re-
veal large, shiny badges. Something about the uncon-
scious, automatic gesture was reassuring, Kelly
thought. It spoke of competence and experience.

Some of the tension went out of Jase as he stepped forward and scrutinized first the badges, then the men.

The slim, dark man said, "Detective Brewster."

His partner, taller, with medium-brown hair, nodded a greeting. "Detective Gunnar."

The dark one asked, "Are you Mr. Whittaker?"

Jase nodded.

"Matthew L. Whittaker?"

"No. I'm Jason, his son."

"May we speak to your father?"

"What about?"

"Something to do with his car," Detective Brewster said vaguely. "Your father, please, Mr. Whittaker."

"He isn't here," Jase said, opening the gate and gesturing for them to enter. "You'll have to make do with me."

Jase was aware of Kelly's worried glance darting between the two men. Her concern was palpable. He could almost see the dark visions running through her brain. Her overactive imagination was conjuring up thoughts of muggings and accidents, then escalating them to hospitals and intensive care units. She'd soon arrive at the morgue, he thought with concern. In an attempt to calm her down, he slipped his arm around her waist and drew her close.

It was the wrong thing to do. He was immediately aware of how few clothes she had on, and that the two men were eyeing her with more than official interest. His first thought was to tell her to go into the house and stay there. His second was that she wouldn't do it. His third was to tell her to go into the house and cover herself from head to toe. His fourth was that the only other item of clothing she had was her bathing suit, which would be going from bad to worse.

Knowing that she would be mad as hell, and that he'd hear about it later, Jase decided he was left with only one alternative: he had to very obviously stake his claim.

Leading the men to the covered patio table, he pulled out a chair for Kelly and waited for her to be seated. When she was settled and looked up at him, he bent forward and kissed her lightly on the lips. Seating himself beside her, he solicitously tucked her hand in his. Just in case the two men hadn't received his message, he said blandly, "This is my friend, Kelly Lyndon." The almost imperceptible pause before the word "friend" erased any remaining doubt. The two men nodded politely, and Kelly's eyes glittered with rage.

Knowing he'd be lucky if she didn't turn every dog in the kennel loose on him, he turned his mind to the business at hand.

"Now," he prompted, "what's this about my father's car, and why are two detectives handling it? I thought they saved you guys for the big stuff."

Kelly's hand stiffened in his. He wasn't doing a hell of a lot to comfort her, he thought in disgust, noting the fear that once again darkened her eyes.

Brewster's voice brought him back to the present. "We got word from down in the San Diego area of an abandoned car. It was traced to your father. And that's why we're on the job," he said matter-of-factly. "His name is well-known in this city and since men in his financial bracket have their own particular set of problems, we're just checking it out."

In addition to his own unpleasant jolt of surprise, Jase felt Kelly's fingertips become icy. He immediately followed her panicky train of thought to kidnapping, ransom and international terrorists. Oh, hell, he thought wearily, life is hard enough to handle without deliberately making it worse. How does she survive with that imagination?

"So exactly what have you got?" he asked.

Brewster pulled out a worn notebook and flipped through some pages. "Yeah, here it is. They found it down around Lake Cuyamaca."

"Lake *what*?" Kelly asked involuntarily.

"Cuyamaca," he repeated absently. He rattled off a license number. "Minor damage."

"Damage?" Kelly's voice was faint.

"Crumpled fender. Nothing serious, but not too many people walk away and leave a brand-new Corvette. A red one."

It wasn't until Jase heard the make of the car that he realized how tense he had been. Now, he released a long, deep sigh. "I think there's been a mix-up. My father owns a silver BMW like the one you passed in the driveway. Our tastes are quite similar," he added irrelevantly.

"I wish that was the case," the detective said regretfully. "But we checked it out and three days ago, Mr. Whittaker traded in the BMW for the Corvette."

Jase looked at him in disbelief and wondered aloud if they were talking about the same man. He told himself, though, that a red Corvette was just one more uncharacteristic event added to three weeks of craziness. It was no more unbelievable than hearing that his father had almost decked an executive at a company function, or run off with an unknown woman, or encouraged that same woman to dance on a tabletop at a famous hotel.

The tension in Kelly's hand had progressed to her arm and was probably paralyzing the rest of her body. He phrased his next question carefully. "Do you have reason to suspect that there's more to this than a fender bender?"

"Nothing beyond the fact that most people wouldn't abandon a new top-of-the-line Corvette," the detective answered dryly. "Plus the fact that your father hasn't reported his car missing." Then he posed an inquiry of his own. "When did you last speak to your father, Mr. Whittaker?"

"Seventeen days ago," Jase answered precisely, after a long moment's thought. "At that time he left on vacation. And, although I haven't personally spoken to him, he's left almost daily messages on my answering machine."

"Have you had any reason to believe that your father's messages aren't . . . genuine?"

"None at all." Jase's calm response did not cover Kelly's frightened gasp.

Brewster examined Kelly's appalled expression with interested eyes.

"Miss Lyndon's mother accompanied my father on the trip," Jase said quietly. He inwardly sighed in exasperation at the resentful glare she aimed in his direction.

Some twenty minutes later, the two men left, seemingly satisfied that there was no reason for further investigation. Jase agreed to take care of the car and to let them know if any trouble developed. He turned from the gate, braced to face Kelly's wrath. It was a good thing he was prepared, he thought, because she was furious.

"How could you do it?" she exploded.

"What?" he asked, distracted by the vivid flash of her eyes.

"*What?* What do you mean, *what*? Pulling that macho, possessive act, that's what. I thought you were going to pin a sign on me that said, 'Possession of Jase Whittaker.'"

That's exactly what I did, honey, he thought complacently, keeping a blandly attentive expression on his face.

"And my mother," she added with renewed fury, "how could you tell them that she was with Matt? You made it sound like...like..."

"Like what?

"Like she was a...a..."

Seeing that she was momentarily preoccupied with finding adequate words to blister him with, Jase gingerly turned her back to the table.

"No one is making any moral judgments about your mother," he said. "I had to tell them, Kelly. If something *had* happened, they needed to know that two people were missing."

Kelly looked up at him, a wretched expression spreading over her face. Clever, Whittaker, real clever, he thought in self-disgust, as she turned and quietly walked away.

Following her to the side of the pool, he stood behind her and wished that he'd had more experience in comforting a woman. Hell, he thought, agitated, any at all would help.

"Kelly?"

"What?" she asked in a whisper.

"Look at me."

She shook her head and continued staring down at the pool.

Jase reached out and grasped her shoulders, gently turning her to face him. For one heart-wrenching moment, he wished he hadn't. Silvery tears were sliding down her cheeks and dropping on her yellow knit shirt.

Following an instinct as old as man, Jase drew her to him. One arm around her shoulders held her against his warmth while his other hand cupped her head.

"Don't be nice to me," she wailed, stiffening in his arms. "I can't stand sympathy." The latest word ended in a hiccup.

"Shhh," he said, tightening his grip on her and touching his lips to her shiny hair. Hot tears slid between her cheek and his bare chest. Jase murmured soft sounds into her hair, smoothing back the tendrils that curled around her face.

Finally, Kelly raised her head and mumbled an embarrassed "Thank you. I think I'm a little scared," she admitted, her eyes wide and serious. "What if something really has happened to them?"

Jase led her over to an old-fashioned glider. After seating himself, he tugged Kelly down into his lap. She settled her head in the hollow of his shoulder and heaved a tremulous sigh. "What if they're hurt? Or what if—"

"They're not," he interrupted firmly.

"But—"

"Come off it, Kelly. Use your head!"

She lifted shocked, protesting eyes to his.

"Remember how fast bad news travels," Jase reminded her. "If they had been killed or injured," he said in a hard voice, ignoring her startled jerk, "we'd have been notified. If they were run off the road by some crazies and held for ransom, we'd have heard from the kidnappers. And I find it hard to believe that they're both wandering around with amnesia. With all that in mind, plus the daily reports on our answering machines that are driving us nuts, I can't find much to worry about."

A rush of relief lightened her expression and he felt the tension leaving her body. She had one last question. "What about the car?"

"I don't know," he replied thoughtfully. "But the way they've been running around," he said with a sudden grin, "I wouldn't be surprised if they finally landed somewhere and decided to sleep for three days and didn't know the car was gone."

"Or they're on a cruise to the Orient and someone stole the car from the parking lot," Kelly suggested lightly.

"Or in a lighthearted moment, my father gave it to someone who just walked away when it ran out of gas."

A comfortable silence fell between them. It was broken when Kelly reached up and kissed Jase on the cheek. "Thank you. You have a definite talent for this kind of thing, Whittaker," she said softly, trying to keep the mood light.

"For what?" he asked.

"For comforting waterlogged women. You must have had a lot of practice."

"Not exactly," he hedged, looking surprised. Well, I'll be damned, he thought blankly. Must have been the body heat. Sure as hell couldn't have been my technique.

Kelly shifted on his lap, totally relaxed, letting him take her full weight. The casual trust of her movement reminded him of something. For a moment, the elusive memory remained just out of reach. Then he remembered. The day in her office when she had stood next to Trent, their bodies touching with with unselfconscious familiarity. He had envied their closeness, wanted her confiding body within the circle of his arms.

Later, Jase remembered, he had been fool enough to warn Kelly not to get too comfortable in his presence. Fortunately, she seemed to have forgotten, because she had just shifted her shapely bottom on his lap and eased back, resting her head on his shoulder. And he was, he realized with surprise, perfectly content with the situation. It wouldn't always be this way, but right now he'd take her anyway he could get her.

"What about the car?" At the quietly spoken question, his eyes met hers.

Until he answered her, he hadn't realized that his decision was already made. "I'm going to drive down. I'll get the car fixed and see what I can find out."

"When do we leave?"

"*I* leave tomorrow."

"Not without me."

"Not this time, honey. I'll probably be gone several days."

"I have it on good authority," she told him quietly, "that when Whittaker and Lyndon travel together, they do it in separate rooms."

"A precedent has been set?"

She nodded serenely. "Exactly."

"I'll think about it."

"Good. Get me home in plenty of time to pack."

Jase glanced down at the smiling woman in his arms, stunned by an overwhelming impulse to hoist her over his shoulder, take her into the house and drop her in the middle of his large bed. He wondered if the lazy smile in her eyes would become one of feminine hunger as he slowly removed her clothes. Yes, he decided, it would. When the time came, she would be all the woman he had ever wanted.

"You're awfully quiet," she commented. "What are you thinking about?"

Caught off guard, Jase looked at her blankly. There's a limit to honesty, he reminded himself, rapidly organizing his scattered thoughts.

"I'm getting a tad impatient with our parents and wonder if you're feeling the same way."

Her quick response surprised him. "Yes, I am. I started on this chase because I was worried about Mom." She shot a hesitant glance up at him. "I, uh, didn't know if she had been coerced into going, and had all kinds of crazy thoughts. But all her messages have finally convinced me. After we check out the car and make sure they're okay, I'm coming back home and getting back to work."

She had succeeded in surprising Jase—mainly because he had arrived at exactly the same conclusion. One last trip, then Matt was on his own. If Abby was anything like her daughter, he thought, then neither one of the Whittakers had anything to worry about. The only thing that had puzzled him right from the beginning was why Matt occupied one room and Abby another.

But then he decided, with another quick glance at Kelly's determined jawline, that the Lyndon women apparently weren't the type to be forced into a relationship or anything else. And he knew that when Kelly finally came to his bed, he wanted her to be as hungry for him as he was for her. If it was going to take separate rooms to bring that about, then so be it.

"Jase?"

"Umm?"

Kelly eyed him warily. Jase was getting that "Me man, you woman" expression again. "I think I ought to get going."

"No rush," he said calmly. "We haven't had dinner yet."

"If we're leaving early in the morning, I have some things to do."

His hands spanned her waist and he hoisted her to her feet. "Dinner first, then I'll take you home," he promised, following her up.

Relieved at his brisk tone, she trotted beside him.

The kitchen was a dream, she decided—almost as nice as her own. The almond tones and sleek cabinets were made even softer with oak trim and plants on the window ledge. Track lights focused on the work areas, she discovered, playing with the light switches.

"Those aren't toys," Jase told her, taking her hand and leading her to the refrigerator. "Salad stuff is down there."

"Okay, okay." She opened a cupboard, looking for a large bowl and found a spice rack built inside. "Look at this! Who designed this kitchen?" she demanded. "I bet it was a woman."

"You win," he said over his shoulder. "Trudy, our cook, had been making plans for years. When we remodeled, she was ready."

"She ought to go into the business," Kelly said.

"Don't even mention it. By doing the kitchen the way she wanted, we managed to keep the best cook in all of California. Lifetime contract."

"You guys really know how to wheel and deal, don't you?"

"We big-time business types are always on our toes," he agreed complacently.

Under the influence of Jase's good-natured teasing, Kelly's natural high spirits asserted themselves. She poked in drawers, wandered into the solarium, returned to offer unwanted advice about grilling steaks, and lost the wary look in her eyes. By the time the steaks were ready and the table was set, she was just as comfortable with him as she was with Mike.

Which just went to show, she decided later, staring open-mouthed in response to Jase's outrageous question, that you just can't trust these big-business types.

"Well," he prodded, "when?"

"Whittaker," she said, dazed but game, "when are you going to get it through your thick head? I am not going to bed with you."

"The whole point is," he explained, kindly, "you need a goal. With your business background, you understand that. Once you have a goal, things get simple. You just direct all your energy toward it."

"You're crazy," she said conversationally. "You know that, don't you?" At his look of innocent interest, she added, "You keep that up, and I'll turn Mike and all the dogs loose on you."

"Come on, Kelly," he prompted, "state your goal."

The gleam in his eyes, she decided with relief, was as much amusement as unadulterated sexual invitation. As long as he wasn't beating his chest and making serious macho noises, she'd play his crazy game.

There was a long pause while she gathered her thoughts. "Okay, my immediate goal is to spend the next few days in your presence and out of your bed."

"Every good businessman or woman also needs long-term goals," he informed her.

"I have a bunch—personal, professional, whatever. None of them include jumping in your bed."

Jase neatly aligned his knife and fork on his plate and raised the napkin to his mouth. His tone, in contrast to the gleam in his eyes, was objective. "To work well, a goal should be specific and positive. Yours," he politely pointed out, "are vague and negative."

"All right," she said promptly, "all of my future goals are specifically designed to keep you out of my bed and me out of yours." She smiled in anticipation, leaning forward. "Is that better?"

He paused, considering her words. His lids dropped lazily to conceal the expression in his eyes. "You're getting close, but you're missing the spirit."

Now what? she wondered. "Should I get out my pom-poms?" she asked, busying herself with cleaning off the table.

He rose to help her carry the dishes to the sink. "No. You just have to put yourself in the other person's shoes for a while."

She rinsed the dishes and he transported them to the washer. "What if I have," she asked thoughtfully, "and I decide that I still prefer my viewpoint?" She tidied the sink and turned to him with a look of expectation.

"Then," he said calmly, lifting her into his arms and heading for the living room, "you have to consider the strength of your opponent."

"Jase! Put me down!" she yelped. "We're supposed to be having an intellectual conversation here, not comparing biceps."

He dropped down on the sofa, holding her in his lap. "Sometimes goals and understanding don't work," he admitted. "When it reaches that point, all you have left is clout. You have to admit that right now I seem to have the upper hand."

At that point, Kelly wasn't sure which hand was upper. Both of them were doing an effective job of holding her in place. Obviously she was going to have to outthink the blasted man.

"Superior strength is an advantage," she acknowledged, "but there are some situations where it isn't a deciding factor."

He surprised her by agreeing. "You're absolutely right." Dropping a swift kiss on her upturned lips, he added, "But it's surprising how having it at the beginning of a situation makes it unnecessary to use it later on."

"I never thought of it that way," she admitted, letting her muscles go limp.

His grip loosened automatically. "You didn't?"

It's now or never, she decided. With an agile twist, she rolled out of his arms to the far end of the sofa. "Nope," she said with a grin, "I certainly didn't."

She rose and straightened her shorts. "Jase, I really have to get home. Besides, all this talk of business strategy has nothing to do with the situation at hand. What we really need to discuss is what they're up to."

Jase surged to his feet and stood beside her. "If I were in my father's shoes, I'd be working like hell to get your mother into bed."

"Jase! We're not talking about you; we're dealing with your father, a gentleman."

He draped his arm around her shoulder and turned her toward the door. His casual words came softly from over her head. "I did mention that we have similar tastes, didn't I?"

Chapter Eight

"You mean to say that you're just going to sit here and do nothing?" Abby looked at the reclining man in astonishment.

"Yep." He opened one eye and squinted as a beam of sunlight worked through the overhead leaves and settled on his face.

"You're not calling the police?"

"Nope."

"Matt, it doesn't make sense. Nobody, not even people who have far too much money for their own good, refuses to report a stolen car." She watched in exasperation as he calmly hitched his straw cowboy hat down over his forehead and settled back with a satisfied sigh.

"We don't need a car right now," he pointed out in a reasonable tone. "We're both tired of traveling. We just want to explore the area on foot. Right?"

"Right," she grudgingly admitted. "But there's something decadent about refusing to tell the police that your car's been stolen. Especially when it's so pretty," she added wistfully.

Matt tilted his hat farther down on his face, hiding a grin. She was getting restless, he noted with satisfaction. His frugal Abby was beginning to chafe under the strain of watching him spend money. Reminding himself that few transactions rested on a single issue, he decided that if he couldn't win Abby by charm alone—and that had been doubtful from the beginning—then he'd have to rely on her puritan work ethic. A woman hell-bent on reforming a man used up a lot of energy, and that energy had to come from somewhere, he reasoned. If he was lucky, it would be transferred from the bank that bolstered her resistance.

How could she be so crazy about a man who drove her to distraction? Abby wondered. What she said was, "You can be very annoying, Matthew Whittaker."

He nodded. "Yeah, I know. Isn't it a good thing you're finding out before you marry me?"

"Why would I want to marry a man who squanders money and lets brand-new cars disappear without a word?" she asked with a frown.

"Because you're crazy about me?" he asked hopefully.

Her brows arched in inquiry. "Do I look crazy?"

Matt reached out for her hand and brought it to his mouth, kissing each finger with great thoroughness. "Abby, the real world is waiting out there for us," he said simply. "Business is out there, and thieves and *police. I don't want to join them any sooner than I have to. I want to stay in this world, with you, until you marry me and we can face them together."*

The simple words silenced Abby. Dear God, she thought in utter panic, it's not fair. A woman in love loses her defenses so easily. This man was a zillionaire, with a life-style that she couldn't even comprehend. And she—Abby swallowed, realizing what she had just admitted—she was a woman in love.

The next morning, Kelly looked out the window just as Jase drove up. She didn't linger to watch him, even though it would have been a nice way to start the day. She was trying to be disciplined, to correct a nasty habit she had recently developed—that of standing around looking at Jase. Besides, she was late.

It was early, the morning air still cool, but she was behind schedule. It had been long after midnight when she'd finally tumbled into bed. She had called Mike to tell him she was taking off again, and written a note to put on her neighbor's door telling of her absence and requesting aid for her plants.

And nothing was going right this morning. Annie sensed change in the air and was sulking, three telephone calls from early-rising mountain people had eaten up thirty minutes, and she still had her case to pack.

After pulling her bag out of the hall closet, she dashed back to meet Jase at the door. "Hi," she said breathlessly, "I'm almost ready. Have a seat. I just have to throw some things in my case, take this note to my neighbor's, catch Annie, and lock the house." She was still talking as she leaned over to pick up her case.

Before Kelly straightened up, a long, warm arm reached out, snagged her waist, and pulled her back against a long, warm body. Then Jase turned her around and enveloped her in a long, warm hug. The tension drained from her as the silent man held her against him.

"Good morning," he said quietly.

"Good morning."

"Better now?"

She took a deep breath. "Uh-hmm."

"What can I do?"

"Catch Annie and hang onto her."

Jase cast a wry look downward. "I don't think that's going to be a problem. She seems to have attached herself to me."

Kelly looked down in surprise. "So she has. It takes her a while, but when she finally makes up her mind, she's a friend for life."

"Kelly," he said, his tone clearly indicating that she should do something, "Annie's drooling on my boots."

"Annie," she informed him with a smile, "has no halfway measures. She either snarls or drools."

Muttering something Kelly was glad she didn't hear, Jase bent his head and kissed the tip of her nose. "I'll handle Drooling Annie and secure the house. You pack and deliver the note."

While she pulled clothes out of drawers and the closet, she called, "I don't know why you insisted on driving up here to get me. You should have let me meet you at your house. I could have dropped Annie off at Mike's on the way."

"I wanted to get started before noon," he answered from the kitchen.

"But you had to get up a half-hour earlier to do it."

"And you got to sleep a half-hour later. A fair exchange." He stood in the doorway, watching her haphazard method of packing with interest. "Everything's locked. Need any help?"

"No, thanks." Kelly knew he was itching to upend the bag and start packing all over again. Neatly, this time. Too bad. She didn't go over to his place and supervise his packing, did she? Pushing with one hand and zipping with the other, she finally closed the case. "Ta-da!" Turning with a flourish, she ignored his wince and headed for the door.

"Why do I get the idea that you like mountains?" Jase asked. It was midafternoon and they were in the middle of the San Bernardino National Forest.

"Isn't it heavenly? I've never had such a lovely drive to San Diego."

"It's different," he agreed. "I've never gone by way of Big Bear Lake."

"You don't mind, do you?" she asked anxiously. "You said we'd probably have to wait until tomorrow to get the car. That's the only reason I asked if you minded traveling on side roads instead of the freeways."

His silence did nothing to alleviate her tension. "You gave me the map," she said defensively. "You told me to navigate."

He considered her statement thoughtfully. "I guess I did. It's been quite an education. I'd never thought of going to San Diego by leapfrogging through the different national forests. What's next?''

She consulted the map. "We go through the San Jacinto Mountains down to the Cleveland National Forest, then bingo, Lake Cuyamaca.''

"And probably not a city with a population over one thousand all the way," Jase muttered. "What was the name of the last town we passed?''

"The one with four hundred and twenty-nine people? I don't remember. It's not on the map.

"I'm beginning to feel like I'm in the Twilight Zone," Jase said, examining the surrounding hills with a city dweller's suspicion of unlimited open space.

"If it makes you feel any better, there's a sign of civilization ahead.''

"Where?''

"That van." Kelly pointed to a scarred and battered van pulled over to the side of the road.

"Looks like he's in trouble. He might need some help." Jase eased up on the accelerator, then drew up behind the large vehicle. "Whatever he's doing doesn't seem to be working.''

Kelly eyed the green monster nervously as it lumbered forward a few feet, shuddered and died. "Jase, we're awfully close to him.''

"There's not a hell of a lot of room to park on this curve," he pointed out, applying the emergency brake and twisting around to check the road behind.

"Jase, I don't think this is a good idea," Kelly began. Her words backed up in her throat as the van was seemingly overtaken with a violent case of hiccups. "Jase?" she said questioningly, as it rocked back and forth. Suddenly, it emitted a rumbling roar, belched out a cloud of black smoke, and shot backward. *"Jase!"*

"What the hell?" By the time he turned, it was too late. With a sickening crunch, the van settled where the front of the BMW had been. Then, with a rattling sigh, it died.

Jase's language was not the type that ordinarily accompanied a eulogy, Kelly thought. But it did match that of the wiry blond teenager who shoved the van door open and jumped down. He took one look at the crumpled, sleek silver car and mouthed a phrase that was succinct and decidedly Anglo-Saxon.

"Are you all right?" His face tight with concern, Jase ran his hands over her shoulders and arms. At her nod, he released his seat belt and opened the door. "Wait here," he said briefly.

Kelly nodded again, only too happy to remain in the car. If the look on Jase's face was any indication, the young man gloomily surveying the mess was in for a bad time. In fact, she decided, Jase's expression, which was probably the one he used to intimidate boards of directors and competitors, was a bit like using a cannon to get rid of a gnat. And entirely unnecessary: the boy was already terrified.

With the windows closed, Kelly couldn't hear a thing. Once she viewed Jase's controlled anger and the boy's abject misery, she decided that she preferred it that way—until Jase asked several questions and tilted his head, waiting for an answer. When he got it and his expression changed to baffled frustration, she opened her door. The kid looked like a typical, terrified, inarticulate teenager. Jase probably needed a translator.

The boy hardly looked old enough to have a license, she thought, and sincerely hoped that she was wrong. Joining them, and listening for a moment, she could understand why Jase looked confused.

"We won't get anywhere in this today," he told her grimly.

The boy nodded in gloomy commiseration. "It's thrashed," he agreed.

Jase touched a tire with his boot. "What a mess."

Nodding again in agreement, the boy mumbled, "Wasted."

"Why the hell didn't you look in your rearview mirror?" Jase exploded. Then, after a quick, disgusted survey of the van door, he added, "Why the hell don't you *have* a rearview mirror?"

The boy's gaze slid to the door and returned, settling on a button of Jase's shirt. "I hear you," he said feelingly.

Kelly reached out and touched his arm. Meeting his startled hazel gaze, she said, "Hi, my name is Kelly. What's yours?"

Responding to her smile the way a puppy does to a kind voice, he turned to her with a hopeful expression. "Allen, uh, Al Sanders."

"Do you have a driver's license, Al?"

"Yeah, sure." He patted his back pocket, then pulled back an empty hand with an alarmed look.

"Maybe it's in the van," Kelly suggested.

"Uh, yeah." He dived inside and rummaged around, searching for it.

"There's something the matter with that kid," Jase stated with a puzzled look. "He hasn't managed one intelligible sentence since he crawled out of that van."

Kelly swallowed the mirth that bubbled in her throat. "You're just used to the young executive types who concentrate on upward mobility and discuss stock options," she told him briskly. "Give him a chance. Once you stop scaring him to death, he'll probably have plenty to say."

"Here it is." Al returned, flourishing a card. He handed it to Kelly, hoping, obviously, for another smile. Kelly passed the card to Jase, who handled the details with a minimum of fuss, and returned it.

"You *do* have insurance, don't you?" Jase inquired in a positively menacing tone.

Al swallowed nervously and nodded. "The minimum," he said.

"Of course. What else would you have?" Jase said dryly.

"What are we going to do about the car?" Kelly asked.

Before Jase could respond, Al said, "I can pull you into town."

"How?"

"With a rope."

"Great!"

Jase interrupted the duet, directing a quelling glance at Kelly, before he turned his attention to Al. "Let me see it."

"Sure." Al leaped back into the van and emerged with a scruffy length of rope that wouldn't pull a bicycle without breaking. Seeing it suddenly through Jase's eyes, he mumbled, "I guess it's not such a good idea."

Jase urged Kelly farther off the road as a car sped by. "We'll have to call a tow truck."

Obviously hoping to salvage what he could from the situation, Al again offered to help. "I'll drive you into town. You can call from there."

Jase opened the trunk and pulled out their bags, then secured the car. Touching Kelly's arm, he turned to the van.

"It's kind of messy," Al explained hesitantly, before opening the door. "I wasn't expecting company."

Jase leaned in for a better look. The seats, all but the driver's, had been replaced by a thick foam pad. The walls were plastered with garish posters. Grimly, he tossed in the two bags and turned to help Kelly.

Whatever else happened in her life, Kelly knew she would never forget the sight of an austere Jase sitting on the floor of a van, leaning against a poster of a sweaty rock singer with purple hair.

"Here we are." Al stopped the van and jumped out with all the irritating vigor of extreme youth. They stood before a white, two-storey house with green trim.

"Exactly where is 'here'?" Jase asked dryly.

Al told them the name of the town and, at their blank expressions, said that he wouldn't be surprised if they hadn't heard of it. It wasn't on the map.

"Exactly how big is this town?" Jase asked with foreboding.

"You mean population?"

Jase nodded, clearly expecting the worst.

"Two hundred and thirty-seven. Or is it six?" Al wondered aloud. "No, still seven, because old Mr.

Magruder died last week, but Penny Milton had a baby yesterday. Still thirty-seven.''

Controlling himself until the census report was finished, Jase asked, ''Is there a gas station in town?''

''Sure.''

''Will you take me there?''

If Jase restrained his exasperation much longer, Kelly thought, he would soon pop a blood vessel.

''Sure,'' Al said helpfully. ''But it won't do any good.''

Jase took a long, deep breath and asked mildly enough, ''Why not?''

''Because it's closed.''

''It's only five o'clock, for God's sake!''

''That right,'' Al agreed. ''That's when Mr. Boot-zig closes.''

''Doesn't he have an emergency number for towing calls?''

Al shook his head. ''Doesn't need one.''

''I'm going to hate myself for asking, but why not?''

''Doesn't have a tow truck.''

''Then why the hell did you bring us here?''

Al pointed over his shoulder. ''This is my house. I thought you could use the phone. The next town has tow trucks.''

Jase said evenly, ''Why don't you just take us to a motel and we'll call from there?'' He watched a peculiar expression spread over Al's young face and sighed. ''Let me guess. There isn't a motel in town.''

''Right,'' Al said, relieved. He turned away from the sight of Jase's grim face. ''I thought maybe you could stay here until you get things straightened out," he told Kelly.

"That's very nice of you, Al, but we couldn't just walk in on your parents."

"Oh, that's okay," he said blithely, "they're gone. Won't be back for a week."

"Gone?" Jase asked in a choked voice.

"But it's all right, Mr. Whittaker," Al said earnestly. "They'd want me to do it. And it's a big house. We've got an extra room." His eyes turned to Kelly, dropped to her bare ring-finger, and grappled with the complexities of modern arrangements. "Rooms?" he asked uncertainly. His gaze swiveled back to Jase, watching his face set in grim lines. "Room," he decided.

"Rooms, plural," Kelly said, taking pity on him.

"We'll use the phone," Jase said decisively, "and worry about the rest later.

Al opened the front door and pointed to a table in the living room. Jase took out a credit card and sat down by the telephone. Kelly followed Al into the kitchen.

"Where are your parents?"

"They went away for a few days to recover from my sister's wedding. They knew they wouldn't get any rest around here. Dad said if they could find a place that didn't have phones, that's where they would stop."

"And left you alone?" Kelly couldn't conceal her surprise.

Al grinned. "He didn't mean it. They called the first night and told me how to reach them. Besides, how old do you think I am?"

Good question, Kelly thought. If you didn't have a driver's license, I'd say about fourteen. "I'm not very good at guessing anyone's age," she said tactfully.

His answer surprised her. "Seventeen. Old enough to be left alone for a week. Anyway," he added honestly, "Mom told everyone in town they were going, so two hundred and thirty-six people are keeping an eye on me."

"And what would they say if they knew you invited two perfect strangers to stay in your house?"

"I won't tell them," he said calmly, as he pulled a package of hamburger buns out of a drawer. "If anyone asks, I'll say you're friends of the family."

Kelly smiled at his willingness to perjure himself. "And what will your folks say when they find out?"

His level gaze was surprisingly serious. "They would expect me to help you. They're going to kill me when they hear about this, so any points I can rack up will help." Pulling dishes out of a cupboard, he asked, "Are you hungry?"

"Starved. Why do you have five thousand frozen hamburger patties in here?" she demanded, inspecting the freezer.

"Because that's all I eat when my folks are gone."

"Don't you ever get tired of them? Silly question," she said, reading the answer on his face. While she pulled out a handful, she asked about the bedrooms. Minutes later, sleeping arrangements settled, the two of them began cooking dinner.

Jase stood quietly in the doorway. "What's going on?"

"You're just in time to slice the onions," Kelly declared. "Our first meal in our temporary home," she added. "I've accepted Al's gracious invitation. Hope you like hamburgers."

A few minutes later, Kelly and Jase watched with awe as Al demolished his third hamburger and reached for a fourth. "Al," Kelly asked suddenly, "what did you mean earlier when you said your folks wouldn't get any rest around here?"

"The city fair," he said thickly, swallowing. "Tomorrow. Every year, the city celebrates its anniversary with a big shindig. Lots of booths with crafts and stuff, lots of food and entertainment. People come from all over." He grinned at Jase. "Population shoots way up for a day."

The telephone rang and Al jumped up to grab the kitchen extension. "Hi, Martha." He covered the mouthpiece and hissed, "Lady across the street." Reaching out a long arm, he snagged a potato chip and popped it into his mouth. "Yeah. They're friends of the family," he said, grinning wickedly at Kelly. "Yeah. They didn't know Mom and Dad would be out of town. They came up for the fair.... Gee, I don't know.... Okay, I'll ask them."

Kelly eyed him suspiciously when he replaced the receiver. "You'll ask us what?"

He looked around for any remaining potato chips, finally settling for a huge glass of milk. Dragging a napkin across a white mustache, he said, "It's no biggie. Martha's in charge of the workers. She said since Mom and Dad are gone, you might have some extra time on your hands tomorrow and thought you might like to work in one of the booths for a while."

"Is there anything else you forgot to tell us?" Jase drawled.

"I don't think so," Al said, "but there's something...no, never mind."

Jase sighed. "But what?"

"Well, I've been thinking about the accident."

"And?"

Al took a deep breath and plunged in. "You must have seen that I was having trouble. Why did you pull up behind me? I never would have hit you if you hadn't been so close!" He finished in a rush, his tone as aggrieved as his expression.

Kelly eyed Jase's blank astonishment and said with a low laugh, "Al, don't you have a girlfriend you want to call, or something?"

The boy followed her gaze, zeroing in on the blend of complicated expressions crossing the older man's face. "Yeah," he agreed cautiously. "I think I do. I'll be in the living room if you want me."

Jase's narrow-eyed stare followed him through the door. "That...*whelp*. He must be an only child."

Kelly giggled. "As a matter of fact, he has three sisters."

"You notice that there are no younger siblings," he pointed out gently.

Kelly defended her protégé spiritedly. "He's a good kid. His parents have done a fine job with him." Changing the subject with a wave of her hand, she asked, "Did you get a tow truck?"

A sharp, exasperated sigh escaped him. "The closest place I could find was about forty miles away. He was almost as bad as the guy up here that closes at five. He said as long as the car wasn't blocking the road, there was no hurry. He'd be along some time tomorrow. And, for an extra charge, he'll come into town and pick us up and take us to a car rental."

Watching Kelly stack the dishes, he added, "I couldn't call home to check my answering machine."

"Did you forget your remote-control gadget?"

He nodded a disgusted affirmative.

"I've got Mike monitoring mine. I'll call him in a while and see if there's anything new."

Jase carried some glasses to the sink. "I'll help you with these. By the time we're through, maybe Romeo will be off the telephone."

"He's a good kid," she repeated.

He muttered a reluctant, "If you say so."

"Good news!" Kelly found Jase in the living room and dropped down beside him on the sofa. She had used the extension in the kitchen to call Mike. "Where's Al?"

"Out on the front porch, talking to some friends. Come here." He tugged, encouraging her to scoot closer and rest her head on his shoulder. She felt so good, so right, so...perfect.

"Don't you want to hear what Mike told me?"

Jase looked at Kelly, his eyes on the sweet curve of her lips. It had been hours since he'd held her, touched her. Too long. He felt like a starving man at a—no, damn it, not a banquet. Anything but that!

"Jase, are you listening to me?"

"Uh-hmm. Mike. Good news." The only good news he was interested in was hearing her settle for one room. And he wouldn't quibble if she put her hand in his and walked up the stairs to that room, softly closing the door behind them.

"The car was stolen!"

That's what it would be, he mused, time stolen from the real world. Time behind that closed door to bring her close, to feel her soft curves melt into the planes of his body. To slowly ease off that knit top and see what frothy bit of nonsense covered her full breasts.

"Mom said they never went south because of the car. But it's been warm—"

Her warm, silken body, fragrant with some light, floral scent was a constant temptation. He wanted to run his hands, his lips, from her toes to her warm, full mouth. He didn't want much, he mused. Only to escape for a while into a—

"She said the whole trip has been like a dream."

—dreamworld where she would look up, eyes heavy with longing, and whisper—

"Two rooms, Jase! They're still in two rooms."

Hours later, Jase was in his room, alone. It wasn't working, he admitted. He was no closer to having Kelly in his bed than he had been three weeks ago. At any time he could have forced the issue—without forcing Kelly. He had kissed enough women to know when one responded. And she did, with fire and longing and sheer feminine enchantment. His sudden grimace was one of self-mockery. Kelly Lyndon—although, God knows, it had taken him long enough to figure it out—was the woman he had been waiting for all his life.

And what was he trying to do? Rush her into bed. He had told her from the beginning that that was where he wanted her. Right from the first, he had pictured her, tousled and love-softened, in his bed. For a night, two nights, three. Whatever he could have, for as long as he could keep her.

Now, he knew that it wasn't enough, that something was lacking. And he had a bone-deep feeling that it was permanence. Several nights or several weeks weren't enough. Damned if he would share her fire, fan the embers to a flash point and turn her loose in the world. No, he wanted it all for himself, for all time.

He wanted the whole works. He wanted Kelly Lyndon to become Kelly Whittaker. He wanted love and marriage, home and hearth. He wanted children, her children. Even after an evening in the company of that young pup, Allen Sanders, he wanted a family.

Jase Whittaker knew the business world. He understood that changing goals called for different tactics. He was astute enough to realize that he was going to have to stop pushing Kelly and present her with a good, old-fashioned courtship. That was it, he decided sleepily; flowers, candy, and real honest-to-God, go-out-for-dinner-and-dancing dates. Maybe two weeks of that would do it.

Chapter Nine

I can't stand it!" Abby tugged at Matt's arm and brought him to a standstill outside the antique store. "If I see you whip out that credit card one more time, I'm going to do something drastic."

He looked down, intrigued. "Like what?"

"I don't know," she admitted finally, after giving the matter a great deal of thought. "But I'll think of something."

"You wanted the book, didn't you?" He tucked her arm comfortably in his and headed back toward the inn. "After all, it's not every day that you find a book about your old hometown. Especially one that's been out of print for eighty years."

"Of course I wanted it. But that's not the point."

"What is?" he asked lazily, amused by her fire-eating expression. Yes, this slothful life was definitely getting to his energetic love.

"The point is," she muttered, *lowering her voice and glaring at a portly man who was almost treading on their heels, "that I should have paid for it."*

"Can't I buy the only woman in my life a gift?" Matt asked whimsically.

Abby pulled her arm from his, coming to a halt in the middle of the sidewalk. She sighed and raised her eyes, obviously seeking inspiration from above. "All you've done since we left Fresno," she pointed out in a determinedly reasonable voice, "is buy me things. You've paid for my rooms, my food, my transportation, my—"

Trying not to grin in the face of her utter exasperation, Matt interrupted her, striving for a wistful tone. "Abby, I've spent years earning money, and had nobody to help me enjoy it. Now—"

"That's a bunch of stuff and you know it," she broke in with a look of obvious disbelief. *"You've probably had women falling over you all your life."*

"What makes you say that?" he asked, his eyes gleaming with genuine interest.

"Because a recluse wouldn't have developed such a—" Abby broke off, damning her impulsive tongue. She wasn't about to add still another weapon to his already impressive arsenal by admitting that she found his charm absolutely devastating. "But that's beside the point," she said, *trying to regain the ground she had lost when he'd strayed from the subject.*

Her startled gaze flew to the man behind them, who was responsible for still another interruption. Unable to pass them on the narrow walk, he was irritably clearing his throat. Before she could do more than glare at him in annoyance, Matt slid his arm around her waist and urged her forward. "You don't want to bother the poor man with our personal problems, do you?" he murmured.

"I don't give a damn about that poor man," she said, not bothering to lower her voice. "I'm simply trying to make you quit spending money like a drunken sailor."

"Do you have any suggestions?" he asked politely, steering her into a coffee shop and leading her to a corner table.

"A couple," she admitted, as the waitress bustled up with menus.

"Such as?" Matt eyed her speculatively, wondering at her suddenly harried expression.

"Everything is so expensive," she burst out.

Matt examined the menu with surprise. "I think it's quite reasonable."

"Not the food, idiot. The lodging!"

Matt leaned back, distantly aware of the blood thudding heavily in his veins. Dear God, he wondered blankly, was this maddening, exasperating, thoroughly enchanting woman trying to tell him the one thing in the world that he wanted to hear?

Noting that his menu had suddenly acquired a tremor, he placed it carefully on the table. Drawing in a long, unsteady breath, he said, "So you think my spending habits are out of hand? That I should retrench?"

"Absolutely," she replied with relief, not expecting him to be so reasonable. "And I'll help."

"How?" The succinct question brought her eyes up to his.

Abby swallowed dryly. "Well, for starters," she finally replied, "this morning I asked the maid to transfer my things to your room."

If it had been necessary, Matt would have slain dragons to remove the anxious uncertainty that suddenly flared in Abby's eyes. Fortunately, no such drastic action was required. He placed her menu on the table and led her outside. "Woman," he muttered, "you sure pick your places for important announcements. Let's go."

"Where?" she asked, not really caring. The invitation gleaming in the depths of his eyes told her all she needed to know.

"Back to our room to start saving money."

"Kelly, are you decent?" Jase stood outside her door with a cup of coffee.

"Go away. It can't be time to get up."

He opened the door, appreciatively eyeing the nicely rounded form beneath the rumpled sheet. "I've got coffee," he tempted, sitting on the edge of the bed.

One blue eye opened cautiously. "With cream?"

He nodded, enjoying the warm, drowsy look of her.

"Oh, Lord, I've died and gone to heaven." Kelly stretched luxuriously, severely testing his new, self-imposed discipline. "What did I do to deserve this?" The bed bounced as she sat up with a jerk and rolled to the other side, heading for the adjoining bathroom. Jase steadied the mug as she muttered, "I've got to brush my teeth so I can enjoy this. Don't go away, I'll be right back."

Go away? he thought, listening to the sounds of running water and a briskly applied toothbrush. Not on your life, lady. Placing the mug on the nightstand, he turned to face the door, wondering with sudden curiosity what Kelly slept in.

"What the devil have you got on?" he inquired, as she opened the door. She looked like a child clad in a giant's castoff clothing. She also looked as sexy as hell.

Kelly looked down in surprise at the shirt that hit just above her knees and had "87" stamped on the front and back. "It's a football jersey. I've worn these to bed for years."

Hopping back into bed, she pulled the sheet to her waist and smiled when Jase handed her the coffee. "Thanks. You're spoiling me, and I love it."

"The shirt?" he prompted.

"Oh. It goes back a long time, to when Mike started playing. He was my idol and I loved wearing his shirts. In order to keep me out of his things, he had one made for me with his number on it. Now, it's just a joke. Every year he has a new one made for me, but it always has the same number." Grinning, she said, "Now you've seen the extent of my alluring nightwear."

Fighting what admittedly was irrational jealousy, Jase forced a smile in return. He wasn't crazy about seeing her in clothing that reminded her of any other man, even a cousin. And did she have any idea, he wondered, exactly how alluring she *did* look? She might think she was a scruffy version of the kid next door, but in a man's eyes, she was delectable. There was something exciting and decidedly stirring about a woman wearing a man's shirt, especially when the only thing it covered was the woman herself.

Kelly finished the coffee and returned the cup to Jase. "Thanks. That's a great way to start the day. What's our schedule for today?"

He groaned. "Don't ask."

"What do you mean?"

His aquamarine gaze slid lazily over her face. "You called Martha last night and volunteered our services for the festival today, didn't you?"

"Who, me?" she asked innocently. "Would I do that without asking you?"

"Don't push your luck," he advised, carefully placing the mug on the nightstand and turning to face her.

"You don't understand, Jase," she said hurriedly, a bit nervous at the amused determination on his face. "This is a perfect chance for me to check out another small-town fair." Tension hummed through her as he planted his large hands flat on the mattress, one on either side of her.

"I want to see how they lay out the craft areas and the food booths," she plowed on. "You do remember that I'm organizing the fair at home, don't you?" Her voice rose a notch as he leaned toward her.

"I haven't forgotten a thing," he assured her. His warm breath brushed her cheek as he continued. "But you'd better hustle if you expect to get in any comparative snooping. Martha has us scheduled to sell balloons from ten to twelve. From twelve to two, you sell beer and I make hamburgers. Then, just for a change, from two to four, we get to deliver prizes to the game booths."

Kelly lifted her eyes from their total concentration on the neck of his knit shirt. A shirt, she noticed, that was bare of little feet, alligators or any other form of status advertisement. Of course, a shirt that was stretched over Jase's muscular frame needed no other ornamentation, she thought wildly. Her startled gaze collided with the marauding masculinity of his and froze for a long, breathless moment.

"How do you know?" she asked feebly.

"Because Major Martha brought over our work schedule at the crack of dawn." Jase absently leaned forward and kissed her on the tip of her nose. "I wonder if anyone has ever reported that woman to the labor board. We don't get a break or time off for lunch."

Kelly released her pent-up breath in a soft whoosh as Jase moved back, resting an elbow on her raised knees. She was absolutely *not* disappointed that he hadn't followed up on all that masculine maneuvering, she told herself bracingly. She hadn't really expected to be kissed silly. Not much.

"It's obvious that you've never worked at one of these things," she said briskly. "You snatch a bite to eat when you can. And you don't get breaks."

Frowning at a sudden thought, she asked, "What about the tow truck. How will the man find us?"

"I tried using that ploy," Jase admitted, leaning against her legs and resting his cheek on his fist. "It didn't work. Once Martha learned that we weren't an emergency case, she called Dex and told him not to come until after five. Dex," he said gently, answering Kelly's mute query, "is Martha's boyfriend. He's also the driver of the tow truck."

Kelly laughed, a low gurgle of amusement that seemed to fascinate the man at her side. "Poor Jase.

This trip has been quite an experience for you, hasn't it?''

He nodded gravely, a thoughtful expression on his face. "I've learned a lot," he agreed. "More than I expected."

In one smooth movement, he surged to his feet, pulling the sheet with him. "You'd better hustle if we're going to make the rounds before we go to work."

With a flash of long slim legs, Kelly exploded into action as soon as he closed the door behind him. Using a lot of water and very little makeup, she was soon ready to tackle her hair. The braid, she decided. It was her usual hot-weather decision. Her hair had a natural wave, which she frequently blessed. The most it ever needed was a blow dryer and a brush, but during the summer a braid was both practical and cool.

She pulled green shorts and matching knit top out of her case. Two minutes later, she finished tying the laces of her white tennis shoes and opened the door.

Jase heard her light tread on the stairs. "That was fast," he said, turning as she entered the kitchen. His sudden, dark frown startled her. "Is that all you're going to wear?" he demanded.

Kelly looked down at her outfit, puzzled. "What's the matter with it?" she asked in honest surprise.

"There's not enough of it," he said succinctly.

"Jase," she said carefully, "it's summer. It's probably going to be close to a hundred today. Every woman out there will have something like this on."

Al walked through the door, oblivious of the tension in the room. "Are we going to eat here, or grab some doughnuts down there?"

"Here," Kelly said definitely, moving around Jase to the refrigerator. She could feel his dark gaze following her as she moved around the room, but she refused to look up. "Al, you set the table and Jase can make the toast." There was nothing wrong with her clothes for heaven's sake. The subject, as far as she was concerned, was closed.

Less than an hour later, the three of them stepped out of Al's van and walked to the tree-lined dirt road that housed the fair. Al left for parts unknown and Jase followed Kelly. What he wanted to do was restrain her with a tug on that sassy, sexy braid, buy a muumuu that was on sale at the first booth and drop it over her head. What he actually did was stay by her side with an expression of taut challenge on his face and intimidate most of the male population.

Kelly, flitting from one booth to another, asking questions and jotting down information, thoroughly enjoyed herself and was unaware of the grim apparition stalking slightly behind her.

It was going to be a long day, Jase decided grimly, aware of the covert male glances veering in her direction. And it was. Clutching a handful of bobbing balloons and followed by a trail of masculine admirers, Kelly resembled nothing so much as a brilliant comet. She, in turn, scowled as Jase passed her, surrounded by a gaggle of women.

From two to four, Kelly did a land-office business selling beer. Jase, busy at a grill in the next booth, looked up once to say, "I don't see you selling any to the women."

"That's because they're all waiting in line to buy hamburgers," she snapped.

The last two hours, they worked together in a large room overflowing with prizes for the game booths. Jase left briefly and returned with a cardboard box full of hamburgers, fries, and two cups of beer. Away from their various admirers, they munched amiably, handing out boxes of junk prizes when runners appeared from the various booths.

"I don't think I'm ever going to eat another hamburger," Jase said, peering suspiciously between the buns.

Kelly took a healthy bite and mumbled, "Fortunately, you worked in the booth, so at least you know what went into these."

"Why do you think I'm so concerned?" he asked wryly, grinning as she abruptly stopped chewing.

"I hope you're joking," she said, slowly swallowing.

"Would I kid about a thing like that?"

After they were released, thanked by Martha and briskly ordered to enjoy themselves, they wandered around eating frozen bananas, looking for their young host. They found him in a booth applying makeup to the faces of delighted youngsters.

He looked up with a proud grin. "What do you think?" he asked.

Kelly looked down at a beaming little redhead who had been transformed into a gruesome monster. "Marvelous! So you're the one responsible for the gallery of horrors running around here?"

Al's grin became, if that was possible, even wider. "What do *you* think, Mr. Whittaker?"

"You have a definite flair for the macabre," Jase equivocated.

"Thanks," Al said dubiously. "I think."

"How much longer are you going to be here?" Kelly asked.

Al eyed the ragtag line of youngsters. "A long time," he decided. "This is free, so the kids just keep coming."

"Free?" Kelly asked with professional interest.

"Martha's idea," Al said laconically as he smeared purple goop on a little boy's face. "Keeps the little suckers busy while their folks spend money."

"I've got to have a long talk with Martha," Kelly muttered thoughtfully.

"Not now," Jase interrupted. "We've got to—"

"Just for a few minutes," she interrupted.

"You can call her when we get back home and talk all day if you want to."

"Do you have any idea how much that would cost?" she asked, horrified.

"You can use my credit card," he added, resorting to blatant bribery.

"Promise?" She grinned up at him. "Scout's honor?"

He nodded.

"Okay." Turning to Al, she said, "You'd better give us your house key. I want to change the sheets on the beds and straighten things up."

"No biggie, Kelly," he said casually. "I'll take care of it."

Kelly eyed him doubtfully. "You sure? You won't leave it for your mother?"

He grinned. "Scout's honor." His smile faded as he looked up at Jase. "Uh, Mr. Whittaker, can I talk to you for a minute? I'm not sure what I have to do about reporting the accident.''

Kelly ambled over to a nearby booth, sternly telling herself to leave them alone, that Al didn't need her protection. Nonetheless, when she glanced anxiously over her shoulder, she was amazed to see the young man beaming with relief. Jase beckoned to her.

As she returned, she heard Jase saying, "We're going back to your house to make some telephone calls. We'll see you before we take off for good.''

"Do you want to use my van?" Al offered.

"Thanks,'' Jase said blandly, "but we need the exercise.''

"What did you say to him?'' Kelly asked as they walked through town. "He looked like he had just been given a last-minute reprieve.''

"I told him to forget it,'' he said shortly. "That I'd take care of the damage.''

"Oh, Jase, what a terrific thing to do!''

He shrugged. "I can afford it. Besides,'' he said philosophically, "he was right. He never would have hit me if I hadn't been right on his tail.''

After unlocking the front door, Jase dug out his credit card and handed it to Kelly. "Why don't you call Mike and see if he's heard any more about your mother?''

She eyed the piece of plastic doubtfully. "I can call collect. That's what I did last night.''

Jase lifted her hand and closed her fingers around the card. "It's easier this way. I'll get my things together while you're on the phone.''

Kelly placed the call and waited patiently through a series of dial tones and buzzing sounds. Mike answered on the fourth ring. "Hi, Mike! I'm calling for today's episode of the missing-persons report."

"You sound chipper," he commented warmly. "I hope you still feel that way when you hear my news."

"What happened?" she asked shakily, almost afraid to listen. "Were they in an accident? Are they hurt? Did they—"

"No, no, and no. Kelly, slow down! They're just fine. There was a lot of interference on the line but I'd swear Aunt Abby said they were going to Lake Tahoe. To get married."

"Married?"

"I think so," he backtracked cautiously. "She finally mentioned that they were staying at an inn in gold country, somewhere between Placerville and Sutter Creek, so I called up there to see if I got the message right."

"Well?"

"I didn't reach her," he said slowly. "The woman in the office said that they checked out of their room yesterday."

Kelly's brows shot up. "Room?" she asked tentatively.

"Room. I think," Mike went on briskly, "that you'd better check Jase's machine."

"Right," she mumbled, "sure. Mike," she ventured, "you did say the *room* they were staying in?"

"Room, as in one," he verified softly before replacing the receiver.

Kelly stared thoughtfully at the telephone for several moments, then called, "Jase!"

He was at her side in an instant. "What's the matter?"

"How far are we from Lake Tahoe?"

"As the crow flies?" he asked finally, "or by way of national forests?"

She eyed him with disgust. "Don't be cute. The quickest way. I think we're going to a wedding."

"Whose?" he asked blankly, wondering if he would ever be able to follow this woman's mental gymnastics.

"Your father's and my mother's."

"No kidding?"

"You don't sound surprised," she commented.

"The only thing that surprises me is that it's taken so long. When is it?"

"I don't know. Mike couldn't understand the whole message. We've got to check your tape. How can you do it without your remote-control whatchamacallit?"

"I'll figure out something. Maybe Trudy is at the house. If not, she lives in the guest house and I'll call her there." He took the credit card she was extending to him. "Why don't you collect your things? This shouldn't take long."

Before she had crammed everything into her case and tugged the zipper around, Jase was beside her. "Mike was right, they're getting married." A grin tugged at his lips. "We've got one small problem, though."

"What?"

"We still don't know when it is."

"Why not?" she asked with a touch of asperity.

He shrugged. "Neither of them mentioned a time."

Kelly blinked. "They didn't?"

"All we know, and that's thanks to Mike, is that they left the Sutter Creek area yesterday. It's not all that far to Tahoe, so they probably drove straight through. They may already be married.''

"I don't believe this,'' Kelly muttered. "What did Matt's message say?''

"That if we wanted to be at the wedding, we'd better hurry.''

"Did he at least tell you where we can find them in Tahoe?''

"Nope.'' Jase's eyes gleamed with amusement. "He forgot that minor detail.''

Kelly gazed upward in supplication. Getting no immediate response, she said to Jase, "It looks like the ball's back in our court.'' Flinging her arms around his waist for a quick hug, she added firmly, "And we've got to think of something clever, because I don't plan to miss my mother's wedding.''

"Do you think we'll make it?''

"God only knows,'' he said with a shrug.

Kelly's gaze swept over the small prop plane they had chartered, settling on the nape of the pilot. She had never been in an airplane this small and hoped he knew what he was doing.

Jase had done something clever, all right, she thought, remembering the past few hectic hours. He'd loped back to the fair, found Martha and stated his problem. She agreed to supervise Dex's handling of the silver car, and within minutes had found someone willing to transport them to the nearest airport. They'd had no difficulty finding a pilot willing to make the flight.

"Well, so much for our plans to go home and get back to work,'' she said with a sigh.

"Hmm."

And so much for that subject, Kelly thought, eyeing him obliquely. He'd been different today, she decided, wondering what was bothering him. Not once had he told her that he planned to scoop her into his bed the first chance he had. Not once had he uttered macho claims. Not once had he warned her about feeling comfortable with him. Not once had he reminded her that he wasn't her brother. And he'd missed about a dozen opportunities to kiss her. She was, of course, totally discounting that platonic nip on her nose early that morning.

Maybe he was tired of the whole thing. Maybe he wasn't into chasing elusive, virginal women. Maybe he wanted to go back to some lush female who trotted into his room and peeled back the king-size covers when he just mentioned the word *bed*. Oh, hell. Maybe he had a sore throat and just didn't want to talk.

Or maybe, she thought with a dismal pang, now that their parents were getting married, he *did* think of her as a sister. Hard to believe, but maybe he could be that stupid.

Hell of a time for the man to turn enigmatic, she thought gloomily. He'd chased her, staked claims and issued warnings about taking her to bed, and now, when she wanted to take him up on some of those promises, he got all silent and moody. There must be a subtle way to let him know that he'd chased her long enough and she was ready to be caught. What she really needed, she decided, was some experience—then she could turn the tables and seduce him!

Jase wondered uneasily what the love of his life was frowning about. He had awakened that morning, remembered his decision of the night before, and predicted that it was going to be a lousy day. And he had been right.

Not that he had changed his mind about the courtship; Kelly deserved that. It was all the accompanying factors that made it such a rotten deal. He didn't object to the flowers or the candy, not even to the dining and dancing.

What bothered him was trying to leave her alone. After one day of trying to back off and give her a little space, he was a wreck. Somehow, this sprite who barely reached his collarbone had wrapped herself around his heart. Her fragrance drove him to distraction, and her laugh was music from the gods. Her legs weren't bad either. He wanted the freedom to reach out and touch her, to unravel her thick, shining braid, to pull her down into his lap and kiss her until she cried out for more. But most of all, he wanted to lie next to her, flesh to flesh, fire to fire, and love her through the night. Or day.

"Almost there," the pilot said over his shoulder. "You can see the lights of the city."

Kelly followed his pointing finger with her eyes. Reaching out to grab Jase's hand, she said, "I hope we're in time. My heart's set on going to a wedding."

Chapter Ten

Abby reluctantly opened her eyes. Bright Tahoe sunlight tentatively investigated the drapes, the sheet had been kicked to the end of the bed, and a man's large, warm hand cupped her breast.

Her brain had no sooner absorbed that last bit of information when her body took over, pouring adrenaline through her veins. Her muscles tightened and she rolled away from the hand, stopping at the far side of the bed. Lifting her chin and looking back, over her shoulder, was probably the most courageous thing she had ever done.

Her eyes widened at the sight of the lean, nude man lying on his side, propped on a bent elbow, staring back at her. The expression in his eyes was a blend of unholy amusement and sheer love.

Collapsing in a boneless heap, she muttered a fervent "Thank God" into the pillow.

"Do you always begin the day this energetically?" Matt asked with a wide grin. *"When it happened yesterday, I thought it might be that you're just not accustomed to finding a man in your bed. Now, I'm not so sure."*

"Two days do not a pattern set," she murmured between several deep breaths. *"And if you value your life,"* she threatened softly, *"you won't hassle me right now. I missed having a heart attack by that much."* She lifted a thumb and forefinger, separated by the width of a sliver, to illustrate her point. *"You have to remember, I'm just a poor, widder-woman, used to sleeping in an empty bed."*

Matt leaned forward, extending a long arm and wrapping his hand around her waist. Tugging gently, he brought her to him until he felt her warmth all the way down his body. He hadn't missed the flush on her cheeks. In the past two days he had learned that while Abby was a woman who gloried in her femininity, she was unaccustomed to intimacy. It had been a long time since she'd shared her life with a man. Her feeble joke had a sound basis in truth; embarrassment had a way of unexpectedly rising up and seizing her. He had, however, found the perfect cure.

He slid one hand down, cupping the curve of her hip. *"My God, you feel good. Like silk."*

"You do too," she murmured, tracing a tantalizing design in the crisp mat of hair covering his chest. *"A much more interesting texture than silk."*

"That tickles," he warned lazily, as her finger slid toward his ribs.

Her eyes widened in mock innocence. *"You mean to say that a little touch like that—"* she brushed her *finger softly down his rib cage, following the narrowing pattern of hair "—bothers you?"*

He raised his hand to the soft swell of her breast, his palm grazing the warm nub at the center. He shook his head in denial. "No more than this brothers you." His slow smile reflected his satisfaction as her breath caught in her throat and she shivered.

He rolled over with her, supporting his weight on his forearms. Looking down at her, he asked, "Did I ever mention that I think Kelly is a terrific kid?"

"Uh-hmm. Several times."

"Where would we be today if she hadn't set up that date?"

"God only knows," Abby murmured vaguely, restlessly shifting her legs.

"I'd like to introduce her to Jase."

"That's nice," Abby said distractedly.

"Who knows, maybe something will come of it."

"Matt! For God's sake! You're driving me—"

Sunlight pounded at the drapes when Abby next opened her eyes. Prodding the bare shoulder next to hers, she said, "Matt?"

"Hmm?"

"Did you remember to tell Jase the name of the chapel?"

A long silence was followed by "Damn!" He sat up, looking down at her with a stunned expression. "Not only did I forget that, I don't think I even told him what day it would be."

She reached up, touching the slight rasp of his beard. "I don't believe it. The man who runs a mul-

tinational corporation, the man Forbes said has a computer for a brain, forgot?''

"Damn," he repeated softly. "He's undoubtedly in town by now, and I have no idea how to find him. Well, at least Kelly will be there.''

"Uh...Matt?''

"Hmm?''

"I forgot to tell Kelly.''

His rumble of laughter blended with her helpless giggle. "You mean Madame Vice-president forgot something that important?''

"I had other things on my mind.''

"Me too," he admitted, tracing her soft curves with his hand.

"What are we going to do?''

His hand stopped, gently kneading the flare of her hip. "We're going to get married," he said evenly.

"But—''

"Abby, it'll be great if our kids are there.'' His shrug was a purely masculine thing. "I'll survive if they aren't. But I won't wait one extra minute for the privilege of calling you my wife.''

"What do we do now?''

Jase looked over, watching Kelly hook the seat belt of the rented car. "Find someplace to stay, I guess. And I don't know how easy that's going to be. Showing up in Tahoe during the season without a reservation isn't the smartest thing I've ever done.''

"Aha! Is this the old it's-too-crowded-to-get-two-rooms-so-we'll-have-to-settle-for-one ploy?'' Kelly asked with interest. I should be so lucky, she thought.

Jase glanced over and smiled at her expression of pert inquiry. Leaning over, he followed up the look with a quick, hard kiss. He deserved that, he told himself, for good behavior. "I'm more direct than that," he drawled, turning the key in the ignition. "When I make my move, you'll know it."

Kelly contented herself with silence and an inward smile. All is not lost, she decided. He didn't say *if*, he said *when*. She was still thinking of all the ramifications of those two little words, when Jase stopped the car at a motel and got out.

He was back within minutes. "All full." The next two stops had the same result. The fourth time he returned, he had a peculiar expression on his face. "Do you happen to know today's date?"

She thought a minute. "July second? Oh, my gosh. This is the Fourth of July weekend! We're going to be lucky if we can rent a pup tent."

Jase stared unseeingly through the windshield, muttering under his breath. Finally, he put the car in gear and melded into the flood of traffic heading for the state line. Minutes later, they were in Nevada.

"You don't happen to own a hotel or two around here, do you?" Kelly asked hopefully. "I'm not really crazy about pup tents."

"Nope. Wrong town. But I think I can find something you'll like."

"Jase, look at that!"

He looked first at her, curious to see what sort of expression would match the utter disbelief of her voice. She was, he noted with amusement, staring out the window with awed fascination.

"Slow down," she commented, forgetting all about hotel rooms. "We just passed the most deliciously tacky chapel I've ever seen. It had animated cupids showering arrows in all directions. And there was another one called Beatitude's Blissful Bridal Bower. They supply the tux and gown, taped music, pictures, flowers and, with an hour's notice, an entire wedding party."

"You made that up," he accused.

"I couldn't," she said simply. "This is beyond even my imagination."

When Jase pulled into the valet parking section of a plush, multistoried hotel, Kelly eyed him uneasily, brought back to the present with a vengeance. "I didn't bring clothes for this kind of place," she protested. Forced into silence while the attendant opened her door, she met Jase at the back of the car and resumed her muttered argument. "Look at what I've got on, for heaven's sake!"

There's one thing you can say about Jase, she decided thoughtfully. He certainly follows orders—when he wants to. His warm gaze made her wonder if she were going to have to do the seducing after all. It slid down, hesitating appreciatively where her blouse and jeans fit snugly, then returned.

"You look just fine," he told her, meaning every word of it. "People in hotels don't care what you wear as long as you pay your bill. Besides," he added, as the doorman threw open the door with a flair that made it a work of art, "the richer you are, the more eccentric they allow you to be."

"But I'm not rich," she wailed softly as he deposited her near an imposing piece of statuary.

"I am," he reminded her with a quick kiss. "Enough for both of us." Whipping out his trusty credit card, he turned to the registration desk.

Kelly stepped to the side of the intimidating sculpture, somehow unsurprised to find a slot machine tucked behind it. She dug into her purse for quarters and dropped them into the hungry mouth of the machine, managing to keep one eye on Jase.

The clerk smiled politely at him, listened attentively, and reached for the telephone. Two minutes later, he was nodding and extending his hand for Jase's car keys. Jase returned with a personal escort, saying, "They'll get our luggage from the car."

"Wait a minute." Kelly collected the five quarters the machine had politely returned.

The bell captain pressed the button for the elevator and held the door open for them.

"What did you do?" Kelly muttered, leaning against the wall as the car shot up, "Buy the place?"

"Almost," he agreed blandly.

Their uniformed escort opened an ornately carved numberless door, handed Jase the key and discreetly disappeared.

"Where on earth are we?" Kelly asked, peering around the imposing room with interest.

"The presidential suite."

"That must be some credit card you have," she murmured, telling herself that she was *not* impressed.

"It's the only thing they had left," he said with a shrug.

Kelly took a quick tour and returned, impressed despite herself. "Jase, do you know there's five bedrooms in this place, each with its own bath?"

"You wanted rooms," he reminded her.

She nodded, averting her face. She had indeed. But that had been a couple of days ago. Before she could think of a nice, safe answer, there was a soft rap at the door. Jase walked over, opened it, held a low-voiced conversation, and returned with a telephone and a directory. Kelly looked at the telephone sitting on a fruitwood desk and asked, "What are we going to do, retreat to the farthest rooms and call each other?"

Jase had the inward look of a man who is solving a problem and has no time for idle chatter. "Those," he said with a sweeping gesture that took in all the instruments in the suite, "are all extensions. This is a separate line."

"And?" Kelly waited patiently for the rest.

"We can make calls at the same time."

"I don't know anyone up here. Who do you want me to call?"

"Hotels."

"But we have a room already. Lots of rooms." Too many rooms.

Jase closed his eyes, muttering something about patience and saints. When he opened them, she wished he hadn't. They remained narrowed and threatening. "You going to clown around all night, or get to work?"

"Work," she decided, choosing the safest option. "What do I do?"

He extended the hand holding a directory. "You take the California side, I'll take Nevada. Call every hotel and ask if our juvenile delinquents are registered."

Kelly sat down at the desk and began dialing.

An hour later, she looked up with a mild complaint. "I've barely made a dent in this list. How are you doing?"

"The same," he said briefly, from across the room.

"Why don't we take a break," she suggested, thinking longingly of the noise and brash glitter of the casino downstairs. "Let's go play the slots for a while."

"No," he said, his tone uncompromising. "Keep calling."

"Did I ever tell you that I am totally and unequivocally addicted to slot machines?"

"Tough."

Jase watched her heave a sigh and run a finger down the list of names. He told himself that he was insane. Right here in this very room he had everything he wanted. He had a woman who was warm and wonderful. A woman who, if the way she came alive in his arms was any indication, was as passionate as she was provoking. A woman his body needed as desperately as it needed oxygen. A woman his soul needed, period. A woman he wanted to take by the hand and lead into any one of those five bedrooms. A woman he wanted to love.

And what was he doing instead? Pushing her to get on with the job. Acting like Simon Legree. Trying to finish the task at hand so he could take her far away from these five bedrooms. Trying to take her back home before he took her, period. Trying to avoid doing the very thing he wanted most to do. Swearing softly, he applied himself to his own list of names.

Kelly looked up just as Jase began dialing. She took in his black frown with a sinking feeling. He looked impatient and disgusted. He didn't look like a man who would be easily seduced—even supposing that she finally figured out how to do it. She bid a reluctant farewell to her role of femme fatale. Apparently it was over before it had even begun.

After another hour, Kelly stood up and stretched. "I think I'll go downstairs and get something to eat." If she sat at that desk one more minute, she'd go stark raving bonkers.

"Call room service," Jase suggested, waiting for someone to answer his latest call.

Only it wasn't a suggestion. It was a flat-out order if she ever heard one. You would think the man didn't trust her to go downstairs and get a simple cup of coffee. She was just about to tell him what he could do with his suspicions when a polite knock sounded at the door.

Turning, just as Jase opened the door, she saw the dark blue and burgundy of the bell captain's uniform. She moved over to the small kitchen, poking around the cupboards, while the two men conversed in low tones. The door closed just as she made a pleasant discovery.

"Look." She brandished a bottle of chilled wine the color of light straw. "I found a bar. Stocked."

"I found something, too," Jase said in a peculiar voice. In his hand were two buff envelopes."

"What's that?" Still clutching the bottle, Kelly stood next to Jase and tried to decipher the writing.

He slanted the envelopes so she could see. One was addressed to each of them. "We've been busting our butts calling every hotel in the county, and they were at this one." Taking everything into consideration, Kelly decided, his language was quite mild.

"This hotel?" she asked, surprised. Although why she should be, she didn't know. Nothing had been simple and straightforward since their parents had met.

He nodded—a short, irritable gesture. It said more than a thousand words.

"Were?"

"They checked out this morning. The night desk-clerk just connected the messages with our names." He handed her the envelope addressed in her mother's writing.

"Wait a minute." She held up the bottle. "I think we may need some of this." She followed Jase to the bar and watched as he opened the bottle with a deft twist. He poured the wine into two glasses, offered her one and returned to the living room.

It only took a minute to read the letters. They looked up at the same time and silently exchanged them. Kelly drained her glass in the silence that followed.

"They're married," she said blankly.

"This morning," he agreed.

Kelly went to the bar and returned with the wine. "And on their way to Yucatán."

"Why, for God's sake, Yucatán?" he asked.

"Pyramids," Kelly said wisely, filling their glasses.

"Pyramids?"

"Uh-hmm. Mom always wanted to see them." Kelly noted with surprise that her goblet was empty again.

"I'm not following them to Yucatán." Jase's expression was stubborn. Obviously he expected an argument.

"I'm with you," Kelly murmured, tilting the bottle toward her glass. "I'll pass on the humidity, heat and bugs."

Suddenly aware of just how many times she had refilled her glass, Jase groaned inwardly as she smiled up at him, shifting back and forth on the cushion, as if, he thought, she was creating a cozy nest for her sweet bottom. It'll be just my luck, he thought gloomily, that her libido sets up a clamor after two glasses of wine.

He rose with a lithe movement and walked across to the window, staring down at the bright lights below. He didn't want her pliable body in his arms because her senses were dulled. Actually, he didn't want her body—pliable or not—in his arms at just this moment.

Who are you kidding? he asked himself wryly. You're afraid to hold her. He had never wanted a woman with such single-minded intensity and found it quite unsettling. You know, he told himself, that if you lay one finger on her, it'll be more than enough to play merry hell with your good intentions.

"Jase?"

"Hmm?"

"What do you want to do now?"

He glanced over his shoulder and eyed her suspiciously. She couldn't possibly be aware of the lethal invitation packed in that one short sentence, he decided after a long moment. The words themselves brought back memories of summertime and kids asking that very question of each other. She neither looked nor sounded like a kid. In fact, leaning against the upholstered arm of the sofa with her legs curled beneath her, she looked exactly like a woman he'd take great pleasure in tossing over his shoulder and hauling into any one of those five damn bedrooms.

Sighing sharply, he said, "What I want to do is quit running all over hell's half acre searching for two people who don't want to be found. I want to go back home and get back to work." And, he added to himself, cram the maximum amount of courting into the minimum amount of time.

Kelly changed position, bringing her knees close to her chest, wrapping her arms around her bent legs. He can't wait to get all involved in work and forget about me completely, she thought miserably, slanting a quick glance at his taut expression. He'd take off those nifty pointy-toed boots that Annie loved to drool on, shuck the sexy Western shirts and become Mr. Executive again. Of course, she admitted fairly, he was just as sexy in the suits he wore at work. Too sexy, she decided darkly, irrationally jealous of the women he encountered during business hours.

Propping her chin on her knees, she asked, "When do you want to leave?"

"Right now," he said absently, his eyes on the snug material following the smooth line of her thighs.

"No," she said firmly, sitting erect, "I'm not budging tonight. It's after midnight and I won't step foot in a car, a van, an airplane or anything you conjure up with the flick of a credit card."

"Tomorrow," he amended, taking a startled glance at his watch. "First thing tomorrow."

"You're really in a hurry, aren't you?"

"Yes."

And that was that. He couldn't make it any clearer. The man simply couldn't wait to wash his hands of the whole miserable mess and get back to his precious corporation. She shouldn't be surprised. She had known from the very beginning that he was out of her league. He was just removing any lingering doubts.

If she didn't say something now, Kelly knew, she'd regret it for the rest of her life. She opened her mouth and nothing came out. Clearing her throat, she tried again. "Jase?"

He sat down beside her, almost throwing her into a state of sheer panic. Good heavens, this was hard enough when he was across the room. The difficulties simply multiplied when he was so close she could count the individual hairs in his mustache, smell his subtle, spicy after-shave, and feel his warmth radiating out to her.

He propped an elbow on the back of the sofa and turned to face her. "What?"

"I don't think I want to go home yet."

"That's okay." His hand went unerringly to her braid, fingers caressing the smooth, shiny strands. "I said tomorrow's fine."

"Tomorrow's too soon," she burst out.

He looked down in surprise. "What do you mean?"

"There's uh, something I want to do, and it'll be easier here than anywhere else."

"I don't want to leave you here on your own," he said with a frown.

"Oh, no," she agreed quickly, "that wouldn't work at all. I can't do it by myself."

"Do you need my help?" he asked, his curiosity stirred by her harried expression.

"That would make it a lot easier," she admitted. *Nothing* will make this easy, she decided, almost wishing she could forget the whole thing.

Jase watched in fascination as the pulse in her throat began beating a rapid tattoo. "Kelly, what are you talking about?" he asked, with a glimmer of a smile.

"What would you say," she asked, throwing caution to the winds, "if I told you I wanted to seduce you?" She held her breath, spellbound by his changing expressions.

"I'd say you're out of your mind," he said grimly. "What do you know about seduction?"

"Very little," she admitted readily. "In fact, the whole thing would go a lot smoother if you handled that part."

"And what would you be doing?" he asked in a voice that hadn't noticeably softened.

"I'm not sure about that, either," she confessed, "but I think—"

"You know what *I* think?" His voice was soft, too soft.

"That you want to try it?" she asked hopefully.

He stood up, bringing her with him. "That you've had too much to drink."

"I have not! Two glasses of wine—"

"Four," he stated evenly.

"Three," she admitted after a moment's consideration. "But, that's not the point we're discussing."

"We're through discussing what we were discussing," he said with sweeping finality, leading her firmly toward one of the bedrooms. "What you need is a good night's sleep. Tomorrow you won't remember a thing about this.'' Wishing he could say the same for himself, he grabbed her case and tossed it on the bed. ''Good night, Kelly.''

What did I do wrong? she wondered, staring at the closed door. She pondered the question as she brushed first her teeth, then her hair. Wondering if he had misunderstood her, she headed for the door.

''Jase.''

He stood facing the window. ''What?'' He glanced over his shoulder. His expression was anything but encouraging.

Kelly walked back into the room. ''I just thought maybe you didn't understand. What I'm trying to say is—''

He was at her side before she could take more than a few steps. Grasping her arm, he led her back into the bedroom. ''I know exactly what you're saying, and I don't want to hear it. Good night, Kelly.''

Once again Kelly was facing a closed door. She was obviously doing something wrong, she decided. But what? Peeling off her jeans, shirt, bra and panties, she mentally replayed the scene. He wasn't a stupid man. And certainly he was an experienced man. So what was the problem? She opened the case, rummaged through it until she unearthed the football jersey and slid it over her head. Maybe he didn't think she was serious.

Once again, she threw open the door and marched into the living room. This time she didn't even get her mouth open before Jase exploded.

''Damn it to hell, Kelly, will you get back in that room!''

With a feeling that she was about to yank the tiger's tail, and not much caring, she shook her head. "No, not until you listen to me. Is that asking so much?"

"It's asking a hell of a lot," he informed her grimly.

"Why?" She sat primly in a straight-backed chair, hands folded on her knees.

"Because, from the time we started this crazy business," he said in a muted roar, "you've talked about your mother, and two rooms, and symbolic acts. Those earnest blue eyes of yours, besides driving me out of my mind, looked out at the world with a special brand of faith and trust. While I was doing my best to get you into bed, you were working your way into my heart." His voice softened as he looked down at her stunned expression. "Honey, I couldn't live with myself if I took you to bed and you woke up in the morning hating me."

"Jase," she said with heartfelt certainty, unable to restrain a foolish grin, "if you would use some of your undoubted expertise, take me to bed, and put an end to this very embarrassing scene, I'll be forever grateful."

He moved close to her, holding her eyes captive with his. "Honey, what the hell brought this on?"

Her tentative smile was reflected in her eyes, revealing far more than she knew. "I changed my mind," she said simply.

Jase gave it one last try, as much to bolster his diminishing control as for her sake. "What about rooms, plural? And your mother? And—"

Kelly's smile was brilliant. "She changed her mind, too."

"What are you talking about?" Jase asked blankly.

"You know the last place they stayed, the inn?"

He nodded.

Kelly held up a forefinger. "One room."

"One?" he repeated, with a reluctant grin.

She nodded. "One."

Jase surged to his feet, picked Kelly up in his arms and swung her around. Dropping down on the couch, with her in his lap, he repeated, "I'll be damned. One!"

"Was it hard?" he asked, suddenly serious.

She had no trouble following his train of thought. "Changing my mind?"

He nodded, watching her expressive face with intensity.

"No," she said thoughtfully. "Because I wasn't giving up any of those other things you talked about. I just expanded my horizons." She grinned wryly. "The hardest part was trying to tell you." Heaving a gusty sigh, she admitted, "I never knew it was so hard to seduce someone."

A chuckle rumbled in his chest. "Damn it, Kelly, I was trying to rush you home so I could court you."

"What a lovely, old-fashioned term," she approved.

"For a lovely, old-fashioned girl." He explained about the flowers, candy, dinner dates and proposal.

"It sounds wonderful," she enthused. "But, can't we do it *after* the wedding?"

Jase cradled Kelly in his arms. His eyes, more serious than she had ever seen them, locked with hers as he asked, "And what about the big seduction?"

Any woman in the world would have recognized Kelly's smile as she whispered, "Can't we do that *before* the wedding?"

Epilogue

Matt," Abby called from upstairs, "did I hear a car door slam? Are the kids here?"

"Not yet," he answered, smiling at the flustered note in her voice. Madame Executive could whip a failing company into shape without blinking an eyelash, but she always had a slight case of nerves before guests arrived. Even if they were her own children.

He stood in the hall doorway, waiting. A simple thing, this business of waiting, he mused. Before Abby's advent into his life, it was something he had done without patience or understanding. Now, he had practically turned it into an art. Not that Abby wasn't punctual. He simply made a point of being early so he could watch her walk down the stairs of the graceful old house.

Abby stopped on the fourth tread from the top, looking down at the man below with her heart in her *eyes. A tiny smile played over her lips.* "What are you doing?"

"Lusting after you," *he admitted with a smile. These days, he seemed to do everything with a smile. Had, as a matter of fact, for two years and twenty-seven days, ever since he first knocked on Abby's door.* "Do you know how incredibly sexy you are when you walk downstairs?"

"Tell me," *she commanded softly, meeting him at the landing and linking her arm through his.*

"Later," *he promised, the glint in his eyes assuring her that he would do exactly that.*

"Right now, we have some celebrating to do."

Abby voiced a mild objection. "I thought we were going to do that with Kelly and Jase."

"We will," *he said calmly, leading her to the fruit-wood bar where he poured two glasses of champagne. He handed her one and lifted the other in a slight, toasting gesture.*

"To two years."

Her eyes met his over the rim of the fluted glass.

"And to the new shark in the corporate world."

Abby smiled complacently. "The Dever merger turned out nicely, didn't it?"

He nodded, a glimmer of amusement lighting his eyes. "How was your lunch with Marge today?"

Abby's laugh was a soft gurgle. "She told me that my replacement as the token woman was an ex-marine. She terrorized Mr. Dever for two years."

"Good," *he said with satisfaction.* "It couldn't happen to a better—"

"I think I hear the kids," *she said hurriedly.*

"Wait a minute," he said. *"Don't put your glass down."*

"There can't be anything else new to celebrate," she objected. *"We've already got it all."*

"I don't think I'm being premature with this." His murmur was barely audible as he lifted his glass for a third time, never taking his eyes off her vivid face. *"To the most beautiful grandmother in the world."*

Two years can change a lot of things, Jase mused. He was lying fully clothed on the bed watching Kelly dress. But there are some things that even time won't change, he decided. For example, Kelly's open-armed approach to life. The corner of his mouth tilted in a private grin as he remembered some of her escapades.

He'd flatly refused to subsidize a shifty-eyed beggar in India whom she'd wanted to bring home. In England, she had tried to start a union for some ladies of the night who had taken her under their wing. Their auspicious meeting had occurred in the English version of the local pokey while Kelly was waiting for him to show up with her bail. He forgot what she had been protesting and exactly how she'd ended up there.

In Scotland, a delegation of local lairds had cornered him, protesting that her attempts to save the salmon were ruining their tourist trade. The small village of Aleut in mainland Alaska would always remember her efforts to set up a community fair. Their contribution, he remembered with a grimace, was some ungodly concoction consisting mainly of whale blubber.

He had a feeling that her shenanigans were about to come to an abrupt halt. "Did I tell you that I promoted Glen Anders?" he asked lazily, watching her hook the front clip of a wispy bra.

"Good. What's he going to be doing?" she asked, slipping on bikini panties, her hand unconsciously lingering on her flat stomach.

"He's now the official traveling man."

Kelly looked up in surprise. "That's *your* job," she pointed out.

"Was," he said complacently. "I'm the boss, remember? I can do whatever I want."

She joined him on the bed, stretching out beside his warm length. "And what do you want to do?" she mumbled into his shoulder.

His hand brushed her hip and caressed the warm, silky skin just below her waist. "I want to settle down and raise a family."

Kelly heard the smile in his voice, but she still wasn't satisfied. "Are you sure?" she asked anxiously. "Won't you miss the challenge and excitement?"

"I never meant for us to keep up that pace," he said with a shrug. "It was only for as long as we enjoyed it, or until something better came along. Now," he said with an almost imperceptible tightening of his hand, "it has."

"And where," she asked, nuzzling her cheek against his shoulder, "are we going to do this famous settling down?"

"Somewhere near your mother, I thought."

It was said so casually, she thought, with a pang of love so fierce it hurt. He just tossed it out, as a mere idea. But she knew he had given the matter a great deal of thought, as he did everything that concerned her.

He had assumed responsibility for her from the very beginning, she remembered with a faint smile. He couldn't believe that her impulsive approach to life was either prudent or safe. He had been determined to wrap her in a net of security and, in her opinion, unrelenting dullness. Her little rebellions had added a certain zest to their life, she decided, smoothing his mustache with a soft finger.

Right from the beginning... She remembered the morning they awoke in the presidential suite. He had listened to her suggestion with increasing grimness.

"No," he stated unequivocally, "I will not get married in a place running rampant with animated cupids or rejoicing in the name Beatitude's Blissful whatever. Absolutely not!"

It had seemed a shame, but he was right, of course. Within two hours they were in a charming little church listening to the beautifully solemn words spoken by a minister. It had been perfect.

She had chosen the location for their wedding breakfast. It was a large hotel noted for its lavish buffets.

"Tell me why you married me," Jase had commanded, trying to ignore the clatter of slot machines in the background.

"Because I wanted access to that remote-control thingamabob you have for the answering machine," she'd answered promptly, neatly cutting a slice of ham.

"Any other reason?" he'd asked with a grin.

"Your credit card racked up a lot of points. I can't wait to get my hands on it. Why else would I marry you?" she'd asked guilelessly.

"Because you're crazy about me?" he had said hopefully.

She had tilted her head and looked at him speculatively. He'd braced himself, expecting another teasing reply. Instead, he had seen the sheen of tears in her eyes.

"You're right about that, Mr. Whittaker," she'd whispered. "I am, indeed, crazy about you."

Now, Kelly looked at her watch and gasped. Rolling away from Jase's warmth, she said, "We're going to be late." She stood up and reached for her dress. As she smoothed the fabric over her hips, she eyed his recumbent form. He looked entirely too comfortable, she decided.

"Did I ever tell you that twins run in the family?" she murmured absently, checking her reflection in the mirror.

Jase jerked, and sat up with a ferocious scowl. "The hell they do! Kelly, I absolutely forbid it."

"I thought you wanted children," she said sadly, eyeing his distracted expression with satisfaction.

"I do. You know I do. But, you're not big enough to carry twins. I won't let you do it!"

"Well, maybe it won't happen," she soothed. "I just thought I'd mention it."

Kelly watched him prowl around the room, muttering and running his hand through his hair. He looked up too quickly and caught the grin on her face. Before she could move, he had her in his arms.

"Twins, huh?"

"There's always a possibility."

"A small one?"

"Very small," she admitted.

"Kelly Whittaker," he shook her gently, "even though you drive me crazy, I love you to distraction."

"I know," she said complacently. "But that's only fair, considering that I'm absolutely wild about you."

And so she was. And so she always would be.

Silhouette Romance

COMING NEXT MONTH

GALLAGHER'S LADY—Brittany Young
Cavan Gallagher spent seven years in prison for a crime he didn't commit. He returned to Ireland for revenge on Meghan's family. His first act: to demand Meghan's hand in marriage.

MAN BY THE FIRE—Victoria Glenn
A husband, children, a home—physicist Sarah Weiss wanted it all. But she was more comfortable with theorems than with men. Until Cal Harriman plucked the doctor out of her think tank and made her a woman.

AN HONEST LOVER—Phyllis Halldorson
Private Investigator Lark hired on as Jonathan Nolan's housekeeper under false pretenses. Soon she found herself wondering how the sexy, intelligent businessman and loving father could be responsible for his ex-wife's disappearance....

THE ROMANTIC AND THE REALIST—Barbara Bartholomew
She was discouraged at the thought of a home on the range, but romance writer Meredith Gage was determined to write a western. Cowboy Gene Crawford taught her everything she needed to know.

MYSTERIES OF THE HEART—Ruth Langan
The manuscript was long overdue, so editor Jenny Mason was sent to "nudge" writer Seth Williams along. But Seth didn't need that obstinate, dedicated little firebrand...did he?

LOVE IS FOREVER—Tracy Sinclair
After five years, Carly didn't expect Jared King to remember her. She had better things to do than play games with Hong Kong's greatest playboy. Only Jared wasn't playing games....

AVAILABLE NOW:

FOUR UNIQUE SERIES
FOR EVERY WOMAN YOU ARE...

Silhouette Romance

Heartwarming romances that will make you
laugh and cry as they bring you all the wonder
and magic of falling in love.

6 titles per month

Silhouette Special Edition

Expanded romances written with emotion and
heightened romantic tension to ensure
powerful stories. A rare blend of passion and
dramatic realism.

6 titles per month

Silhouette Desire

Believable, sensuous, compelling—and
above all, romantic—these stories deliver
the promise of love, the guarantee
of satisfaction.

6 titles per month

Silhouette Intimate Moments

Love stories that entice; longer, more
sensuous romances filled with adventure,
suspense, glamour and melodrama.

4 titles per month

Silhouette Intimate Moments

Love stories that entice;
longer, more sensuous romances
filled with adventure,
suspense, glamour
and melodrama.